STUCK ON VACATION
WITH RYAN RUPERT

By

P.S.Malcolm

Copyright © 2016 P.S. Malcolm

Printed by Ingram Spark

Stuck on Vacation with Ryan Rupert

Cover design by jeshart

Map art by Alina

ISBN: 978-0-9954272-2-8

Second Edition (Published 2018)

Find out more about the author and upcoming books online at psmalcolm.com

to laura h, for the holiday that inspired this book.

CONTENTS

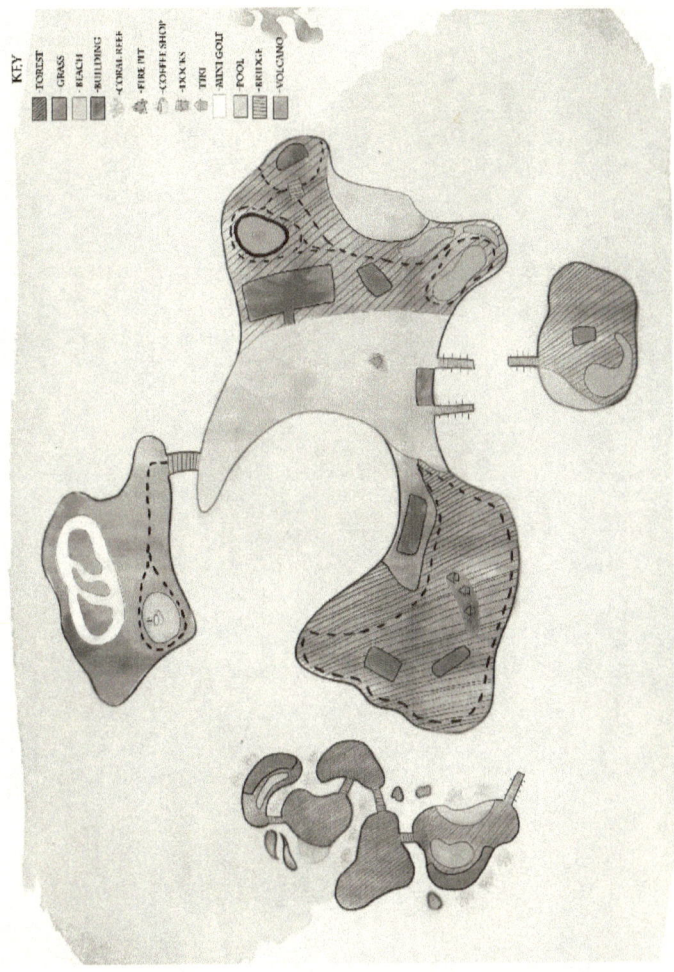

KEY

FOREST
GRASS
BEACH
BUILDING
CORAL REEF
FIRE PIT
COFFEE SHOP
ROCKS
TIKI
MINI GOLF
POOL
BRIDGE
VOLCANO

CHAPTER ONE

A HOLIDAY FROM HELL

Summer vacations are supposed to be fun. They're supposed to be filled with memories of friends and first loves and the relief of being completely free of schoolwork. But clearly some*one* or some*thing* (I personally blamed the Fates) had decided to ruin mine by sticking me on an island for six weeks.

Now, I know what you're thinking: what is *wrong* with this girl? It's summer, and islands are the perfect place to enjoy the sunny days and clear skies that summer brings! They're filled with surf, sand, exploring, and activities. And that's all great if you're someone else.

But not if you're me.

For me, an island is the equivalent of hell. I have a colossal fear of the ocean, and the thing about islands is, well, they're kind of *surrounded* by water. And if you aren't up for ocean-related activities then, well, what good is being on an island? What good is summer vacation if it means leaving all my wonderful friends and spending six weeks trapped with my sworn enemy?

Who's my sworn enemy, you ask? Maybe I should start at the beginning.

It was a beautiful, early summer morning in Tallahassee, Florida. I was very happily skipping through the morning television programs in the family room, lazing around, and preparing myself for a day of chillaxing. But that all changed as soon as my parents entered the room.

"Aubany, we need to talk to you," my father said. He turned the television off, and faced me. His expression was grim; his eyes lacked their usual twinkle, and his mouth was pulled into a thin line. That made me realise it was serious. They sat down with me and proceeded to tell me the worst news of my life.

"Your mother has cancer," Dad said. That sentence alone took me a few moments to process.

"What?" I said weakly. My Mom had cancer? My beautiful, kind and caring Mom? These kinds of things, they didn't happen to people like her . . . right?

Looking at her now, she looked anything but sick. Her fair skin had a healthy glow, her red hair cascaded over her shoulders, and her green eyes sparkled even though, right now, they seemed sad.

My grandmother told me that Mom had looked the mirror image of me in her youth.

"I don't understand," I said slowly, trying to get my bearings. "What kind of cancer? How did this even happen?"

"Sweetie," Mom said gently, putting her hand over mine, "Everything is going to be okay. It's stage two breast cancer, and I'm going to be flying to California to see a specialist."

"A specialist?" I repeated, feeling numb. That sounded daunting.

"I've been getting regular check-ups, but this came on so suddenly, and the doctor here referred us to a professional who has more experience with this kind of thing. We do have a history of cancer in the family, but it's been quite rare and unpredictable along our generations. So, the specialist is going to try and figure out exactly what genes in our family history might be triggering it."

I swallowed hard, blinking back tears. She had to fly all the way to California just for that? And since when did we have a family history of cancer? I'd never heard either of my parents mention it. Did that mean I was going to get cancer too?

I had so many questions, but before I could ask any more, Dad chimed in,

"I'll be going with her."

The way he said it implied that I wasn't coming.

"What about me?" I asked, frowning. Did they plan on leaving me behind?

14

"We don't have the money to pay for all of us to go, Honey," Dad said. "We know you want to be there, but your mother and I need to do this on our own."

"Then what am I going to do?" I asked, and I could feel the hysterics building. Not *only* were they leaving me behind, but I felt like I was being excluded, information wise.

"Well, your Aunt Celeste is busy. She can't take you in. And the cousins are a bit too far away. We can't afford to send you to them either. So we've asked the Ruperts for a favour."

"The Ruperts?" I repeated. They were our neighbours. Josh and Renee were nice enough people, and they had always been very kind to me. Their son, however, was a different story altogether.

Their son was Ryan Rupert. He was a jerk, an ass, and pretty much every other bad thing under the sun. He was a nightmare to be around, and he *hated* me. Lucky for him, the feeling was mutual.

"The Ruperts have kindly agreed to look after you while we're gone," Dad said.

"Oh, great. I don't have to live in their house, do I?" I asked. I really didn't want to have to see Ryan every day. "I mean, I can just stay here - right? They can just pop in from time to time and check on me. I can cook my own meals, and buy my own food. I can get a summer job."

I'd been trying to convince my parents to let me get a job for years now. I'd not long turned 17, and I was eager to start earning some money of my own. Melissa had been working at the record store in town for the past year, and she seemed way more mature because of it. But my parents had insisted that school should come first, and had worried that my grades would suffer with the addition of a job.

"No, Honey, it's more complicated than that," Mom said. "I wouldn't feel comfortable leaving you on your own. What if something happened? And besides, the Ruperts won't be able to check in on you every day because they aren't going to be here."

16

"What do you mean?" I asked slowly.

"The Ruperts already have a vacation planned," Dad said. "And you'll be going with them."

"A vacation?" I exclaimed, horror stricken. "*Where*?"

"To an island. Nula Island," Dad said.

This could *not* be happening. I had to give up my summer vacation, miss out on all the parties my friends were going to throw, to be on some *island* with my sworn enemy?

This was so unfair, and not just because of *that* reason. My Mom was sick with cancer. *Cancer*! Of all the things she could be sick with, and my parents were forcing me to tag along on the Ruperts' family vacation rather than be at her side?

No way. I wasn't going to go.

"You can't make me do that. Come on, you know how I feel about Ryan!" I protested. "And besides, I'm terrified of the ocean. How will I survive on an island?"

"Aubany, please," my Dad said softly. "Don't argue. It'll upset your mother."

I ignored his words. "Upset Mom? What about me? Aren't I allowed to be upset? You do realise what you're asking me, right? You think this is easy for me? To accept that Mom has cancer? To accept that I can't be with her for the next six weeks? To accept that I'm going to be stuck with *Ryan Rupert*? You want me to just nod and say it's all okay?"

"This isn't easy for us either, Aubany," Mom said, looking hurt now. She seemed to understand me completely, and I realised they really had no choice but to do this.

"But . . . isn't there another way?" I said, my voice wavering. Maybe I couldn't stay with my parents, but *surely* the Ruperts weren't the only other option. "Can't I stay with someone else? What about Melissa?" I asked, desperate to dig my way out of this. Melissa was my best friend. Surely I could stay with her, right?

"We've known the Ruperts since you were very little. They are more than happy to look after you. But to ask that of someone else's parents would be too much. We're going to be gone for a long time, and we don't know when we'll be back. It would be unfair to put this on Melissa's parents," Dad said.

I was out of ideas. I felt sort of surreal. I couldn't believe this was happening.

I knew it seemed so stupid to whine about a six-week vacation when my Mom was sitting beside me gravely ill with a disease she could possibly die from. But it wasn't fair, and I just couldn't stop thinking of all the horrible ways this summer could go wrong. I hated Ryan Rupert with every fibre of my being, and having to be stranded on an island with him for six weeks was a nightmare in every sense of the word. Being his neighbour was bad enough. He had already found plenty of ways to annoy and taunt me just by living next to me. On an island there would be no escape. I'd have nowhere to run.

"We're sorry, but this is the only way. We'll call you all the time to tell you how things are going," Dad promised. Mom got up and left, and Dad began to follow her. He stopped before leaving the room and said, "Try not to let this get to you. The Ruperts had a room available so they are kindly paying for you. Try and make the best of it. It's summer, and you get to spend it on an island for free!"

I really wished I could look at this from an optimistic point of view, but nothing was optimistic where Ryan Rupert was involved.

To make matters worse, I hardly had any time to prepare myself emotionally for the trauma this whole experience was going to bring me.

A few days later I found myself on the doorstep of the Ruperts' house, waving goodbye to my parents as they left for the airport.

I should have run then and there. I should have made up a story to tell Josh and Renee, and lived in my house while my parents were gone. Who would have known?

But instead I rang the doorbell and waited for them to let me in. I heard footsteps, and the door swung open. A petite, blonde woman opened the door, all smiles and perfect peach skin, greeting me with her friendly blue eyes.

"Hello, honey," Renee gushed. "Let me help you with that." She took my suitcase and led me inside.

I'd been in the Ruperts' house a few times before. It was a Spanish-style house, with rounded arches and iron railings. I remembered when we'd been invited to Josh's 40th birthday party. Ryan had had all his friends over and they were in the pool. I'd just gotten my first period for the first time, and I'd worn a white summer dress, having no intention of going swimming whatsoever. But Ryan's friends thought it would be fun to push me into the pool. Thanks to my white dress, their prank had turned into a huge disaster. Ryan had gotten yelled at, but it wasn't enough to justify the humiliation I received when I emerged with a transparent view of my bra and a very obvious red stain on my behind. I'd rushed back home to change and never bothered coming back.

Every other visit to the Ruperts' house had ended in a similar and tragic fashion. It was no wonder I was on edge as I followed Renee into the kitchen.

And who should I run into there but the devil himself? He had his father's messy black hair, his mother's beautiful blue eyes, a strong jawline, and a sexy smile that made all the girls at school swoon. If he wasn't such a jerk, maybe I'd consider him date-worthy, but in this, the land of reality, I'd already accepted that most hot guys *were* jerks. Ryan was certainly no exception.

He was seated at the table eating cereal. I don't know what it was about hot people, but they always seemed to look flawless no matter what they were doing. Even now, as Ryan shovelled cornflakes into his mouth at an alarmingly fast rate, he managed to look good.

"Ryan, can you show Aubany to her room?" Renee asked, reaching over to scoop her keys off the bench beside her. "I have to duck out and grab some last minute stuff from the store before we leave to-morrow."

He smirked. "Sure, I can do that," he said. His eyes met mine, and they already had a look that spelled trouble.

"Thanks, Sweetheart," Renee said. "I'll be back soon. Aubany, you just make yourself right at home, okay? Help yourself to anything you want, Dear," she said kindly, before she left.

I glared at Ryan with my arms folded. Normally, I'd thank a person for letting me stay in their home, but since I didn't plan on showing Ryan any kindness whatsoever, I kept my lips zipped.

He stood up and took his bowl to the sink, then turned to me, grinning.

"So, Aubany—"

"Do not talk to me," I said firmly. "Just show me where my room is and leave me in peace."

"Ouch. What did I do?" he asked in a mock friendly voice.

I narrowed my eyes at him.

"I'm going to ignore you," I declared. I grabbed my luggage and walked past him. He followed me down the hall to the staircase. I began to lug my bag up the steps. It made a loud *thwack* each time it hit a step.

"Would you like a hand?" Ryan offered smugly, leaning casually on the black iron railing.

I snorted. "Like I'd trust *you* with my luggage," I muttered darkly.

I was about halfway up when Ryan said, "I just thought I'd let you know that we're sharing a room."

I stopped in my tracks and turned to face him.

"What?" I snapped.

"On the island, I mean. That's what Mom told me anyway," he shrugged, beginning to climb the stairs. "She said she didn't want to book another room when mine already had two beds, and she figured you wouldn't want to stay with them, so . . ."

This had to be a joke. It was a joke, right? Renee wasn't stupid. She wouldn't let her teenage son and a girl share a room, would she?

"I don't believe you," I said, refusing to let him get to me. He was beside me now, taking my suitcase from me. He lightly touched my hand as he did so, which made me jump and pull my hand back quickly. He carried it up the stairs with ease.

"Hey, where are you going with that?" I cried, racing after him. He took it to a room, that I assumed was mine because, other than the fluffy white towel neatly folded on the bed, it showed no signs of being lived in. Ryan dumped the bag in a corner and turned to me.

"You always assume the worst of me, don't you?" he asked with a smirk.

I glared at him.

"We're not seriously sharing a room, are we?" I asked.

"Hey, it wasn't my idea. I was looking forward to having a room of my own, far away from my parents. But then you showed up and ruined it all."

I gawked at him. He was blaming *me*?

"It's not like I *want* to come on your stupid vacation, okay? I'd much rather be here in Florida than stuck with you!" I spat.

He glared at me.

"Well, I guess we're just going to have to learn to live with each other, aren't we?" he said coldly. He headed for the door, but before he left, he turned to me and added, "Although I'd rather drown myself than ever get along with you."

CHAPTER TWO

A SPLASHY STATEMENT

That night at dinner, Josh and Renee couldn't stop talking about the island.

"Oh, it's going to be so fun, Aubany, you're going to love it," Renee insisted. "There's so much to do, and it's all paid for so you don't have to worry about any of that."

"Oh . . . well, great," I said politely. I was well aware that the majority of activities involved the ocean—and I had no intention of participating in any of them.

"There's swimming, and snorkelling, and they even have a miniature golf course!" Renee continued. "Of course, it's not all on one island. Everything is spread out over four different islands. There are little boats to take you from one to the other."

I almost choked on my spaghetti. "Four islands?" I exclaimed.

"I know, it's exciting!" Renee said, completely misreading my expression. "You and Ryan are staying on the main island. That's where all the shops and pools are, and the dining hall," Renee said. I breathed a sigh of relief. As long as my room was on the same island as the food, then I wouldn't need to go anywhere else that involved trips over the ocean.

"Our room is on the Lanikai Island though, so if you need us you'll have to take a boat over. The trips aren't long. They only take about five minutes each way."

Five minutes on water was too much for me.

"How long is the boat trip to get there?" Ryan asked from beside me. He kept kicking me occasionally, but I was ignoring it.

"Two hours," Josh replied.

Two whole hours? I must have gone pale, because Renee suddenly gave me a worried look.

"Aubany? Are you alright, Honey?" she asked, as I shifted uncomfortably in my seat.

"Um . . ." I trailed off. I didn't want to worry them, but I figured they should probably know of my fear of the sea. On the other hand, once Ryan got hold of that knowledge, he'd have the perfect weapon to make my life miserable. So, instead, I smiled at them and said, "I'm fine. Just a little worried about my Mom."

"Oh, yes. Poor Caroline," Renee frowned, and said sympathetically, "I never imagined something so horrible would happen to that lovely woman. I hope everything goes okay for her in California."

There was an awkward silence after that, and a feeling of sadness spread through my chest. Mom would have landed by now. Perhaps she was on her way to the hotel? I considered calling her after dinner. I wanted to check up on her, and make sure she was okay. But that would mean facing the fact that she *had* cancer, and if I did that I'd probably start crying.

I mean, I wanted to start crying right *now*, in front of *everyone*.

I was *not* about to start crying, especially in front of the likes of Ryan.

I cleared my throat and said, "So Ryan tells me we'll be sharing a room." A part of me still didn't believe him.

But, to my disappointment, Renee nodded and said, "Yes. I just didn't see the point of paying for another room. But I trust you two will be responsible." She was giving Ryan a firm look. I glanced at him and he rolled his eyes.

"Yeah, yeah," he muttered.

"There are two beds though, so it should be perfectly fine," Renee added breezily—like sharing a room with Ryan wasn't an absolute recipe for disaster. "And I've heard your room has a beautiful view of the ocean from the balcony. You can hear the waves at night and everything!"

I grimaced. That was exactly what I *didn't* need.

I quickly finished eating and stood to take my plate to the sink, but Renee stopped me.

"I'll take it, Dear. You can go ahead and take a shower if you want. Guests always go first in our house."

I thanked her and headed up the stairs to my room. I gathered my toiletries, pajamas and the towel from the bed, then went into the bathroom. Their bathroom was as beautiful as the rest of the house. The shower was spacious and had a glass brick wall to the left. The sink and vanity unit was so smooth you could hardly tell where the sink started to dip below the counter. A potted orchid sat in the corner, adding a touch of colour and natural beauty to the room. I quickly stripped down and jumped in the shower.

I felt more relaxed in the shower than I had all day. The feeling of hot water soothing my back muscles was enough to make me close my eyes and hum softly, completely at ease.

Once I'd finished, I stepped out and grabbed my towel to dry off. But when I went to get dressed, I ran into a tiny problem.

My clothes had disappeared.

I'd left them on the vanity, and now they were gone.

A feeling of dread and disgust crept through me. Someone had taken my clothes while I was showering.

Someone had come *in* here! And I was betting it wasn't Josh or Renee.

Wrapping a towel around myself, I marched out of the bathroom and down the hall until I found a door that said "Ryan" on it. I knocked, but immediately cursed myself for it. I shouldn't have to knock when he invaded *my* privacy. Why should I show him any respect whatsoever?

"Come in," called a voice. I threw the door open and shot him a glare. He was lounging on his bed playing video games. He raised his eyebrows at me, pretending to be surprised.

"Well, this wouldn't be the first time I've had a naked girl barge into my room," he said slyly, putting down the controller. I pulled my towel tighter around me.

"I'm not here to play your stupid games, Ryan. Where are my clothes?" I demanded.

"I could tell you . . ." he said slowly. " . . .but it would be so much more amusing to let you search for them." He gave me a challenging look.

"Ryan," I warned darkly, taking a step forward, "It's bad enough that you walked in on me showering. I swear to God if you took even the tiniest peek—"

He scoffed. "Like anyone would want to check you out showering," he said, as if it was the most disgusting idea in the world.

It took all of my self-control not to attack him at that moment. I huffed angrily, turned on my heel, and stormed out of his room back to my own. I quickly found something else to wear—taking a moment to be thankful that he hadn't decided to take the entire contents of my suitcase—and hid my suitcase in the closet for good measure. Then I stood up and looked around.

I didn't particularly want to go searching the Rupert's house for my clothes. I personally wouldn't like it if someone decided to snoop around *my* house. And while I had a perfectly good excuse, I didn't even know where to start looking. The Rupert's house was huge. Knowing Ryan, he had probably spread my clothes out all over the place.

With an annoyed sigh, I crossed to the balcony and opened the glass doors. I was already being tormented by him and we hadn't even left Florida yet! I couldn't imagine what sharing a room with him for six weeks was going to be like. Sadly, I leaned on the railing and looked over at my lonely house next door. How I wished I were over there right now.

I looked down at the Rupert's back yard. Their pool was lit up by bright lights, and the shrubbery surrounding it cast shadows all over the pavement like some kind of artistic portrait. As I looked closer,

I realised the portrait contained lots of soggy looking clumps of fabric floating in the pool.

I gasped.

My clothes!

I raced downstairs and through the family room, past Renee and Josh. I threw open the doors and ran to the pool's edge. I stared out into the water. My poor, innocent clothes!

I reached in and coaxed my favourite Hello Kitty T-shirt over to the pool's edge. A waterfall came pouring out of it as I rescued it from the cold, deadly waters of the Rupert's pool. My clothes and I had endured too many bad experiences within its depths.

"Aubany?" came Renee's voice from behind me. As she reached my side, she realized what I was doing. "Oh my goodness. Are these yours?" she asked. I heard laughing high above me. I looked up and saw Ryan with his head sticking out of his window. He shot me a smirk.

"Ryan Rupert!" Renee bellowed from beside me, her hands on her hips. "You get down here at once and get these clothes out of the pool for Aubany!"

He disappeared from the window. Renee turned back to me.

"I'm so sorry," she said quickly. "I just don't know why he pulls these pranks all the time . . ."

"Don't worry about it," I mumbled. "I'm used to it."

As I tried to squeeze the water out of my T-shirt, I looked out at my satin shorts and black bra that had floated out into the middle of the pool.

Gently taking the shirt from my hands, Renee said, "We'll put these straight in the dryer for you. They'll be nice and clean for when we leave tomorrow morning."

The door opened, and Ryan trudged out towards us. Renee shot me a wink before turning to her son. She stopped Ryan in his tracks as he made his way over to get the pool skimmer, which was leaning against the fence nearby.

36

"Oh no you don't, Mister. You're going to get into that water and fetch them out by hand," Renee ordered.

"What?" Ryan cried.

"You heard me. I don't care how cold that water is," Renee said, folding her arms. "And when you're done you'll bring them to the laundry room. Oh, and you'll apologize to Aubany."

"Yeah . . . what she said," he mumbled obnoxiously, as if forming a proper apology was too hard for him to handle. Then he casually stripped off his shirt and jumped into the pool. I leaned back to avoid getting splashed. I thought that enough of my clothes had suffered for one night.

Renee went back inside, shaking her head and leaving me alone with Ryan. I had a good mind to leave him to it, but I was afraid to let my clothes out of my sight. So I watched him as he swam around gathering them all up and dumping them on the side of the pool. Once he'd grabbed the last of them, he pulled himself out, completely drenched. I had to admit, he looked kind of sexy with all that water dripping off of him and clinging to his hair. But those thoughts soon vanished when he stood up and glared at me for a few seconds. Then he sighed and grabbed my clothes. As he passed me he said, "Cute undies."

I immediately went red, fuming.

"God, you're such a jerk!" I said angrily. Fists clenched, I marched back inside. I couldn't believe him!

When I was safely back in my room, I tried to occupy myself by reading one of the books I'd brought with me, but I was too angry and I kept thinking about Ryan's pathetic actions. Eventually, I ended up turning off the light and climbing into bed. I could hear the light hum of the dryer downstairs, and I could see the pool lights through the transparent white curtains that breezed gently in and out of the room.

I tossed and turned, my fears of the ocean keeping me awake. I felt very alone all of a sudden. None of the Ruperts knew what I was like around boats and the sea. I wanted to pretend like I'd be fine, but I knew I wouldn't. Tomorrow was going to be the worst day of my life.

CHAPTER THREE

DISCOVERING AN ANGEL

The next morning went by very quickly. Renee woke me at the crack of dawn and whisked me down the stairs to eat breakfast, which was cereal. Then we all had to load the taxi up with luggage, check that the house was locked up, and squish into the taxi together. I was practically sitting on Ryan's lap, and we were surrounded by suitcases. The position put us both in a bitter mood.

When we reached the docks, we unloaded the car. I was only too eager to escape from Ryan. I didn't even look at him as I followed Renee and Josh inside the reception to check our luggage. Every time the automatic office doors opened, I got a strong whiff of salty sea air that made me want to vomit. I felt queasy knowing that just outside the door, the ocean waited only a few yards below the pier.

We had to wait half an hour before our boat arrived, so we all trudged out to the pier and found a table. I sat very still and tried not to inhale, but I soon realised that oxygen was vital to survival and I couldn't hold my breath forever. Before long, I had to make an excuse and took a quick walk along the pier in search of new smells to distract me. I found an ice cream stand nearby and hovered near it. It was better than nothing.

I closed my eyes to focus on the smell of ice cream, and I wasn't watching where I was going as I headed for the wall behind the stand. I had intended to lean on it.

I *hadn't* intended to knock someone over in the process.

We both crashed onto the floor. That's when I noticed I'd knocked over a pretty, blonde girl who was looking kind of dazed.

"I am so sorry!" I said, getting up. I offered her my hand and helped her to her feet.

"The world flipped over for a second there," she said, rubbing her head. She looked at me. Her eyes were light grey, and she had the kind of face you see supermodels walking around with.

"Are you okay?" I asked, as I found myself staring at her.

"Oh yeah, I'm good," she said with a laugh. I continued to stare.

"I'm sorry," I said finally. "It's just . . .you're really pretty."

"Thanks," she said with a huge smile. "I'm Savannah!" She offered me her hand, and I shook it.

"I'm Aubany," I replied.

"Aubany. That's a nice name," she said. I noticed we were taking up a lot of the walkway, so I took a few steps back to let people pass. In the process, I backed straight into the railing. I stumbled and gripped the barrier for support, only to look down and see the vast blue ocean beneath me.

I got dizzy.

"Hey, are you okay?" Savannah asked as I continued to grip the railing tightly and shut my eyes.

"I need a distraction," I said, my breathing ragged. "The salt in the air . . .I think I'm going to be sick."

"Salt?" she said. "Oh!" She quickly rummaged through her handbag and whipped out a tiny bottle of perfume. "Give me your hand," she ordered.

I did as she said and she sprayed my wrist a few times. It smelt sweet and a tiny bit musky.

"It's by Taylor Swift," she told me. I brought my wrist up to my nose and took a few deep breaths.

"That's a lot better," I said, beginning to calm down. "Thank you so much."

"No worries," she replied. I gave her a small smile.

"So . . .are you travelling somewhere?" I asked.

"I'm taking a vacation. I've been working for a year and a half and I felt the need to get away, so I decided to just do it!" she said. "Besides, I've always wanted to visit an island."

"I'm going to Nula Island," I told her. "But not by choice."

"No way!" she exclaimed. "I'm going there too!"

My eyes widened. "Really?" I said. "Well . . .do you think we could hang out there?"

"Absolutely," she agreed. Suddenly the world seemed to get a little brighter. Maybe I *wasn't* doomed to spend six weeks in hell with Ryan. Maybe Savannah was an angel sent from heaven to shield me from his obnoxious ways and keep this from being the worst summer vacation ever.

Maybe.

"Well, we'd better start getting in line," Savannah said, pointing over my shoulder. "The boat's arriving."

I saw a tiny speck in the distance and realised she was right.

"I'll catch up with you later. I have to meet up with someone," I told her. We said goodbye and I went off to find the Ruperts.

Ryan hadn't moved from the table, but Renee and Josh had wandered off somewhere. Ryan spotted me and got to his feet.

"There you are!" he exclaimed. "Mom and Dad went looking for you. They were worried because they thought you looked sick."

He paused.

"Actually, now that I get a good look at you, you *do* kind of—"

"I'm fine," I snapped, before he could finish. The last thing I needed was Ryan finding out about my fear of the sea. I didn't know how I would be able to keep it a secret, but I was going to try. I would *not* let Ryan have the upper hand. One wrong move and it was all over!

Ryan shrugged. "Whatever. I just hope you don't ruin this vacation."

I couldn't believe him! Did he *ever* think before he said such rude things? Did he have even a *shred* of kindness or consideration for other people's feelings?

Right after I thought that, he squashed an ant that had been innocently running across the table.

I guessed not.

Renee and Josh appeared in the crowd a few moments later.

"Oh, there she is!" Renee said to Josh. They came over to me. "Aubany, Sweetie, are you alright? You're looking a bit pale," Renee said.

"Don't worry Renee, I'm totally fine," I said, giving her my best smile.

"Well, if you need anything, don't hesitate to ask, alright?" she said. I nodded. They glanced over to the dock.

"Ah. They're starting to board people," Josh said. We stood up and headed over to the ramp. Renee and Josh went first, and Ryan followed.

I hesitated at the bottom of the ramp. The ocean water was sloshing under it, clearly visible through the tiny holes in the metal flooring. Ryan looked back and saw me clutching the railing.

"Come on!" he insisted. When I didn't move, he stopped in his tracks. "What are you doing?" he asked.

"I . . ." I trailed off. "I can't."

"What are you talking about?" he asked, looking annoyed. He started walking back up to me, threading through the people that were beginning to walk past us.

"I don't think I should go with you guys," I said weakly. "You go without me. I'll just get a taxi back home and stay there instead."

"What the heck is your problem?" Ryan said. He grabbed my arm and tried to drag me down but I dug my heels into the metal floor. His tugging caused me to slip and I shrieked, gripping onto the rail for dear life.

Ryan stared at me for a few moments.

"Just relax and don't look down," I closed my eyes and muttered to myself.

"Oh . . . my . . . God," Ryan said slowly. I opened my eyes and saw his excited expression.

"Oh my *God*!" he repeated. "I can't believe this! This is *gold*!" he cried. He raised an eyebrow and smugly said, "You're afraid of the sea, aren't you?"

So much for my ability to keep secrets.

"Please don't do anything to me," I begged. "Please, Ryan. Do not make me go near that water. I am *terrified* right now."

"Oh man, this is going to be so much fun!" he said, an evil glint in his eye. "You, on an island. *Surrounded* by the ocean!" he made big gestures above his head with his hands and kept laughing. "You are *so* coming with us. This is too good."

He grabbed my arm and pulled me again. This time I was too overwhelmed to stop him from dragging me up the railing. Part of me was too busy thinking of the horrible things Ryan was planning on doing to me to process that I was getting closer to the sea with every step. So when I suddenly found myself on the deck of the boat, I freaked out.

"Oh my God," I said, grabbing the nearest stable thing I could find . . . which, unfortunately, happened to be an old man.

The ocean waves were rocking the boat, and I could feel every movement. I felt queasy again, and the loud sloshing sound that kept echoing up from the side of the boat wasn't helping. Just when I thought I was about to lose it, I felt a steady hand on my shoulder.

"Come on," a voice said. Someone steered me inside, away from the sound of the waves and the salty air. The rocking sensation hadn't ceased in the cabin, but it was significantly better than being out on the deck. I looked to my left and spotted Savannah at my side. She was steering me towards a seat. I fell into it, relieved. She took a seat opposite me.

"Here," she said, passing me a water bottle. I gratefully took it and sipped. The insides of my stomach had been churning.

"Thanks," I said, handing it back. She shook her head.

"It's for you," she said. "That boy told me to give it to you."

"What boy?" I asked. Was she referring to Ryan?

"When you first got on the boat you weren't responding to anything. He went off to get you water. Then I took you inside because you suddenly snapped out of it and started to freak out. He passed it to me as we were heading in."

"Which boy? What did he look like?" I asked. She turned around and pointed across the room.

"That one," she said.

It was unmistakably Ryan. But that was impossible. Ryan was a jerk. He'd never do something nice like that for me. He glanced in our direction and his eyes met mine.

He shot me a smug look that said, *Enjoy your freedom while you can, because the minute we get off this boat I'm going to make your life hell.*

CHAPTER FOUR

WELCOME TO NULA ISLAND

I spent the whole boat trip reminding myself where the life jackets were located in case the boat went down. From the moment the attendant had mentioned it, all I could think about was the possibility that we *might* actually need life jackets and that we *could* go down.

I hated boats with a passion. I'd been traumatised ever since I watched *Titanic* when I was younger. Which is why, when the boat finally reached the island, I was out of my seat within seconds and immediately made a beeline for the exit.

"Aubany, wait up!" Savannah called from behind me. I pushed through the people, only too happy to get off the boat. After two hours of being rocked from side to side, the docks didn't seem so bad after all. Sure, there was water beneath me, but I was finally standing on solid ground, and I felt safe again.

However, if there's one thing I've learned, it's that nothing lasts forever. Safety was nothing but a slim glimmer of hope, and it was well and truly gone the moment Ryan stepped off the boat.

It slowly dawned on me that, while Savannah might be my guardian angel, even she couldn't protect me 24/7. And right now she was hurrying off to collect her luggage and find her room, leaving me alone with my worst nightmare.

Ryan had this creepy smile on his face. "You know, I'm still trying to get over how funny this is," he said. "I cannot believe you actually came here, being so afraid of the ocean."

"Well, it's not like I had a choice!" I said firmly. I folded my arms.

"Why didn't you say something earlier? Did you really think you could keep your little secret from me forever?" he taunted. "Oh, I've already thought of tons of ways to torture you. This place is packed with water activities, and my parents are staying on one of the smaller islands, so our chances of running into them are basically zero. You're stuck with me!"

"Don't get too excited. I don't plan on hanging around you long enough for you to be able to pull one of your stunts on me. I plan on staying as *far* away from you as I can for the next six weeks," I replied.

"That's funny, because I had planned to do that too, originally. But now . . . how can I resist?" he asked. He took a step closer and added, "I simply can't leave you alone here."

"Gee, stalker-ish much?" I asked. I began to walk away from him towards the ramp that would lead me off the dreaded pier.

Ryan followed me as I climbed up the ramp. I stopped when I reached the top and stared.

I had to admit—the place was breathtaking.

At first glance, you could see the entrance to the resort up ahead in all its dazzling splendour. There were tall, engraved wooden columns, arches with breezy curtains tied back, flowers spilling over the rooftops and climbing up the walls, and fountains sprouting from the rock pools that lined the path to the entrance.

The hotel's wings were spread out over the four islands, with seven wings in total.

"Come on, Reception's this way," Ryan said, walking ahead of me. I followed him down the path towards the grand building before us. Passing through the doors, I stepped onto weathered wooden floorboards. Past another fountain situated in the centre of the room, a huge desk took up half the space near the far wall.

Ryan checked us in, grabbed two key cards, and handed me one of them.

"We're in the Sea Breeze Wing, room number 309," he told me. We were given a map to follow, and Ryan led us back out of reception.

I studied the map intently, trying to make sense of where everything was. What I'd been told had been right—the island really *was* huge. Luckily, the map sort of doubled as a brochure, packed with hot tips and information, which I took the liberty of educating myself on.

We were literally on the dead center of the island. If we went back the way we'd come, we'd head towards Sea Spray Beach—where the docks were for the dinghies . . . or taxis . . . or whatever they were referred to here. It wasn't anything that concerned me, as I had no intention of traveling to the other islands. I skimmed over that part completely.

If we went south we'd end up at the Tiki Village and the boardwalk, where most of the island's full-time residents lived. Unless I got a sudden urge for overpriced souvenir shopping, that part of the island didn't sound too appealing.

Going north would lead us to the pools and the majority of the island's most adventurous hikes. The brochure described the area as "an explorer's paradise", and claimed it had many secrets waiting to be discovered.

Finally, if we went left, we'd head towards Pualani Island, where the golf course was located.

But just before you reached the bridge that connected Pualani Island to the main island, you'd conveniently end up at the Sea Breeze Wing—a.k.a., my prison cell for the next six weeks.

We began to head that way along the beach, which had a few palm trees scattered here and there, but otherwise was just a big stretch of sand with a few huts toward the end. We passed the surf shack that sat in the middle of the beach and, from that point on, the beach began to get a lot narrower. The sea was creeping closer and closer with every step I took. I crossed over so that I could walk on the other side of Ryan.

"Do you think this is the right way?" I asked anxiously.

Ryan raised an eyebrow at me. "*You're* the one with the map!"

I eyed the water cautiously and bit my lip. "I know . . . I just . . ."

He shot me a smirk and said, "Getting a little nervous, are we? Here, hand me the map then."

I glared at him, ignoring his outstretched hand that indicated for me to pass over the map. "Do you even know how to read a map?"

He smirked, looking amused. "I wouldn't be making snide comments if I were you," he said. "After all, the sea is right there . . ."

I shut up.

We were approaching a set of beach huts that sat by the edge of the sea on a small rocky cliff. The brightly painted doors were surrounded by a tropical garden of leafy green plants and hibiscus flowers. We followed the path until we found our hut, and Ryan slid the key card in the slot. The door swung open, revealing a spacious, bright room. Two queen beds sat against a turquoise wall. They each had white sheets and blue and green, fern-patterned comforters. The pillows were big and white, and there were decorative blue and green pillows everywhere. I crossed the polished floorboards and peered out the glass doors that led to a balcony. The ocean was right there, just as Renee had said. I turned away from it, grimacing.

I spotted a door along the wall between the two beds. I poked my head in the door and saw a spacious bathroom with a glass-tiled shower. Taking a step back and looking around, I also saw a wooden table which held a small flat screen T.V. Next to that was a small kitchen with a mini bar, as well as a coffee maker and tea. The room was air-conditioned, too.

"This is really nice," I said, forgetting that I was supposed to be miserable and that I had just spoken to my mortal enemy.

Ryan seemed to forget that fact, too. "I know, right? It's awesome!"

We both looked at each other, then frowned. We turned away and occupied ourselves by looking around some more. I sat down on the bed nearest the balcony. It had a comfortable mattress with soft, clean sheets. I was about to lie down when suddenly Ryan sat next to me.

"What?" I asked.

"I want this bed," he said.

"Does it matter?" I asked. "What's wrong with the other one?"

He smirked. "This one is more comfortable. Besides, whose family is paying for the room? Mine. So I get this bed," he said.

"Fine," I muttered, moving to the other bed. He followed me.

"I've changed my mind. I want this one," he said, smirking.

"Don't be so immature!" I snapped angrily. "Which bed do you want?"

"How about both?" he asked, smiling.

"Then where will I sleep?" I asked, immediately regretting the question.

"Well, you know, we could always blow up a mattress and throw it in the ocean for you to sleep on," he said.

I narrowed my eyes at him.

"Very funny," I said sarcastically. I gave up. I'd wait for him to go to bed and sleep in whichever bed he didn't sleep in. There was a few minutes of awkward silence, during which I pretended to be very interested in the floor.

"But seriously," he said suddenly, "I can't believe you're scared of the ocean."

"You're not going to let me live this down, are you?" I asked. "Why are you so obsessed with taunting me? Can't you go find some other girl to torture?"

"No," he replied.

"Why not?" I asked, irritated.

He held my gaze, a smirk forming at the corners of his mouth. "Because some other girl wouldn't be you."

I was silent, unsure how to respond. Before I could think about it any further, my phone rang, which rapidly eliminated the sudden . . . *discomfort* that had begun to seep into the air. I jumped to my feet and grabbed my phone from my pocket.

The caller ID read Mom.

"I . . . I have to take this," I said quickly, hurrying out of the room. I was secretly thanking Mom in my head for her perfect timing. I wasn't sure if I could have handled any more of that unsettling conversation.

"Hi Mom!" I chirped, once I was safely outside. "How are you? Did you have a safe trip?"

"We did, Sweetie, thanks for asking," she replied. "I'm sorry I didn't call sooner. I meant to, but we just got so crazy busy! As soon as we got here we had to drive to the clinic and see the doctor, and then we had to check into the hotel which was *at least* another half hour away—"

"Mom, it's fine," I said quickly, before she worked herself up too much. "I get it. You were tired and this was the first opportunity."

"I just wanted to make sure you were okay," she said, sounding worried. "Your father and I feel so bad about having to leave you. We know how much you hate the sea . . ."

I crossed the path outside our room and sat on the rock wall lining the walkway.

"I'm fine. I'm here in one piece, and I haven't thrown up yet, so that's all I can ask for really," I said, trying to be positive about the whole situation. Just hearing Mom's voice was making me more upset by the second. I missed her, and I missed *home*, and I hated that this cancer was the cause of everything that had happened. If she was healthy I wouldn't have to *be* here, and she wouldn't be growing sicker with each passing day!

To be honest . . . I'd just been trying to block it all out. If I let myself get too hung up on it, I'd just put myself in the worst possible mental state, and dealing with the possibility of Mom *dying* on top of Ryan's taunting would only lead to lots of crying and, most likely, a breakdown.

But if I didn't *think* about it . . . if I pretended like she was fine and had just gone to California with Dad for a few weeks . . . then it was one less thing I had to focus on. I didn't know how I was meant to handle all of this . . . how *did* anyone handle these things? For now . . . for now it was easier to block it out. Though I couldn't do it *forever* . . . I could do it until I needed to deal with it. And when *that* time came . . . *if* it came . . . well, it wouldn't be like I had a choice.

"Well, I'm glad you seem to be handling it," she said finally.

I didn't want to talk about our present situation. I wanted to avoid the reality and just talk about *any-thing* else.

The good thing was, Mom and I had the *perfect* relationship for that. We were so close that as soon as I changed the topic, she caught on quite quickly and seemed content to chat with me for a good half hour about all sorts of meaningless, time-filling top-ics. And that was all we needed. We just wanted a sense of normality—a sense of how much we loved each other. I'd almost forgotten that I was on an is-land by the time the conversation ended.

When she hung up, a feeling of loneliness came over me as I realized *just* how much I needed my

Mom right now . . . and how much more I'd need her if she didn't make it home.

CHAPTER FIVE

WRONG ROOM

After my phone call with Mom, I hadn't been willing to go back to the room, so I decided to take a walk along the beach. Now alone with my thoughts once more, my mind kept replaying what Ryan had said to me.

What had he meant by his words? Why had they left me so uncomfortable? Why was the idea of "some other girl not being me" making me feel things I most definitely *shouldn't* be feeling? It wasn't like he was confessing to *loving* me or anything. But the meaning behind his words and the *actual* words he'd used, out of *all* the words he *could* have used . . . they left me incredibly confused.

As I dug my toes into the sand I thought about it further. He could have just meant that I was his favourite victim. That probably *was* what he meant. After all, he hated me. He always had. We'd grown up hating each other.

I didn't even remember how it all started, but, for as long as I could remember he'd gone out of his way to make my life harder. Pulling pranks. Calling me names. Ganging up on me with his friends. I'd learned to ignore it.

Still, it wasn't long before I started retaliating a little. I began to develop a wider, and possibly not very ladylike vocabulary for those oh so *lovely* moments when he'd ride by on his bike and call me something insulting or throw something at me. For a long time I thought it was because of my hair colour, because a lot of the time his comments seemed to be directed at that.

I hadn't seen anything wrong with having red hair—personally, I thought it was a gorgeous colour. But it didn't seem so strange for Ryan to have issues with red hair when so many other people I'd grown up with seemed to have issues with it, too.

One thing I'd learned very early on is that people love to make fun of people who are different. Being a natural born redhead is actually quite rare.

There's so much nonsense surrounding the stereotypical personality of someone with red hair— something I'd never listened to, myself. And watching kids like me grow up getting bullied gave a sense of normality to the idea. At the very least, it gave me a reason to suspect why Ryan disliked me. It also gave me more reason to dislike *him*. I mean, why would somebody—of all things—pick on someone for the colour of their hair? It was so *stupid!*

When Ryan became more creative with his insults and pranks, I realised that maybe it didn't have anything to do with me having red hair. Maybe he just genuinely disliked me for existing. And let me tell you—that wasn't so far-fetched, either. I could name a number of people who hadn't done anything to me, but whose presence I couldn't stand all the same. Don't ask me why—I just knew better than to bully them about it.

I guess my retaliation had led Ryan to believe that I hated him as much as he hated me. (Which, quite honestly, was pretty true. He hadn't given me any reason *not* to hate him.) Our complicated relationship had grown worse and worse over the years—and now, we had to share a room.

Oh, the joy.

I was wandering past Reception when I spotted Savannah. I called out to her and headed her way.

"Hey!" she greeted me. "Ooh, you're looking much better now!"

"That's because the sea is way over there." I pointed behind me and she giggled.

"Aubany, my room is *amazing*!" she said excitedly. "It has a private balcony which looks over the sea, and a jacuzzi tub! Oh, and it has the softest king bed with yellow and orange sheets! Yellow is my favourite colour!"

"What? We didn't get a jacuzzi tub!" I grumbled. I pretended to sulk, and we both laughed.

"So, let me guess. You have a fear of the sea or something, don't you?" she said. I nodded.

"Then what are you doing here?" she asked, looking utterly confused. I explained my situation to her, and she gave me a sympathetic look.

"That's awful," she said when I'd finished. "I'm so sorry about your Mom. And your roommate. Although, I will admit, he looked kind of cute."

"Trust me, he isn't worth your time," I replied.

"Well, I was going to ask you if you wanted to do some activities with me but they all pretty much involve water . . ."

"Don't get me wrong, I would love to do activities with you," I said, "but I just can't."

"It's okay. Maybe we can just go exploring. See what the island has to offer." she suggested.

I decided that was a brilliant idea. It would keep my mind off Ryan for a while and ensure I didn't have to be around him for at least a few hours.

We followed the map so we wouldn't get lost. We walked along a little path that curved around a rock garden, and soon came across a pool area. The summer heat made the idea of a swim very tempting, but I would've had to go back to my room to get my swimsuit. The whole point of taking a walk was so that I wouldn't have to go back and face Ryan, so we simply walked around it.

There were two pools in this area, one smaller than the other. The bigger one had a swim-up bar, and the smaller one—closer to the gardens, had a bridge.

We crossed the bridge and Savannah made us stop so she could check out a hot guy who was diving in. I had to admit, he *did* have a cute face. And seeing him shirtless wasn't too bad either.

Eventually, I managed to steer Savannah away and we headed back along the beach towards the Tiki Village, where all the shops were. Most of it was just souvenir stuff—dolphin bracelets, shell earrings, postcards that cost more than they were worth, and expensive straw hats with pretty ribbons tied around them. There was an ice cream stand nearby and yet another pool (this one shaped like a jellybean).

When our legs got sore from walking, we stopped to sit down—and just talked. Savannah was nineteen years old, from Florida like me, and worked at a modelling agency as an assistant. When I told her I was still in high school, she was surprised.

"You look older than seventeen," she said.

"Everyone says that," I replied.

When it started to get dark, I told her I was going to head back to my room. The island had little golf carts that escorted people around, and I decided to take one rather than trek all the way back to Sea Spray Beach.

When I got back to the huts, I fumbled for my key card, but couldn't find it. Panic swept through me when I realised I'd left it behind in the room.

Dammit.

I took a deep breath to calm down. No biggie. All I had to do was knock and Ryan would let me in. And sure, he'd probably make fun of me or make a stupid remark, but it wasn't such a big deal.

I knocked. When there wasn't any answer, I knocked again. Slowly, I realised he must have gone out.

Now I *really* had a reason to panic. Where had he gone? And how would I get into the room?

I spun around, looking for an answer, when I spotted someone walking down the path dressed in a staff uniform. She looked as if she was in the middle of taking someone's bags to their room.

"Excuse me!" I called. She came to a stop in front of me. "I've forgotten my key card in my room and I'm locked out," I said.

She pulled out the master card from her pocket and slid it in. The door opened, and I sighed in relief. It looked like I wouldn't have to deal with Ryan after all.

"Thank you so much," I told her.

She smiled. "No problem."

I headed inside. It wasn't until I'd taken a few steps that I realized something was wrong. The curtains were closed and there was only one bed, which had clearly been used. The wall was moss green, not turquoise. And someone was in the room.

Changing.

"Oh crap . . ." I whispered. The man turned around, but I was already running out.

"Hey!" came an angry voice behind me as I ran down the path. I ran faster, not looking back. I ducked behind a wall and stood there for what seemed like forever, not knowing what to do.

If that wasn't my room, which one *was*? Where was Ryan when I actually needed him?

Just my luck, a familiar figure walked past right then, with a head of messy black hair and his hands in his pockets as he walked. Speak of the devil.

"Ryan!" I called, walking over to him. He turned around. I saw his expression turn to surprise as I appeared out of nowhere.

"Geez, there you are! I've been looking everywhere. I thought you wandered off and got lost," he said, folding his arms and glaring.

I frowned at him. "Please. I wouldn't get lost. I'm not a kid."

"You could have fooled me," he muttered sarcastically. I was about to snap back at him when he added, "So, why did you call my name? I would've thought that getting my attention would be the last thing you'd want to do."

"Um . . . I forgot my key card," I admitted, turning my head away from him. Technically, I guess I *had* gotten lost by going in the wrong room, but I wasn't about to tell him that.

"That's exactly the kind of thing a kid would do!" he announced.

I glared at him.

He sighed, shaking his head. "What would you do without me?" He pulled out his key card and dangled it in front of me with a smug smile. "Follow me," he said.

I really didn't want to, but there was no point in staying put or running off again. He seemed to enjoy this small moment—when I needed his help. I hated that I had no choice but to rely on him.

He led me down the hall and stopped outside our cabin, which, now that I looked at it, clearly had a different shade of paint.

When I stepped inside, I noticed that Ryan had made himself at home. His luggage was unpacked and his suitcase was pushed up against the wall, out of the way. Mine lay untouched on the far bed, the one Ryan had originally insisted on having. I crossed over to it and began to unpack, just to keep myself busy. Ryan occupied himself by watching TV, and we ignored each other. The silence between us was almost comfortable.

When I'd finished unpacking, I grabbed one of my books and looked around for a place to sit and read. Inside, I would be distracted, but outside on the balcony, I'd get sick from the sea air. I was about to sit down in a chair when Ryan looked up at me. For a moment, I was reminded of his comment that had made me leave in the first place.

"You look kind of miserable," he noted.

I shot him a look. "I wonder why," I replied bitterly.

"Are you always going to be this moody?" he asked, frowning. I ignored him, took a seat, and opened my book to read. "I thought about you being stuck on an island for six weeks with nothing to do, and it made me kind of sad."

I looked up.

"I'm sorry?" I said. I'd never heard him say anything like that before. Why would he be sad for me?

Then I saw the way he was trying not to smile, and the mischievous look in his eyes.

"So I took the liberty of ensuring you wouldn't be sitting around here sulking for the next six weeks," he said. "I booked us to go on a kayaking trip."

For a moment, all I could do was stare at him. Had he *really* just said what I thought he'd said?

"You what?" I asked tensely. "Ryan . . . in case you don't remember . . . I'm *afraid of the sea*!"

"And I plan to use that to my advantage," he grinned. "Besides, I'm doing you a favor. By the end of this holiday, you'll have done so many water-related activities that your fear of the sea will be long gone!"

"I don't *want* to confront my fear of the sea," I said darkly. "I don't want to go anywhere *near* it!" What made him think he could force me to do something like that?

"You can't just sit here doing nothing," he pointed out.

"Yeah? Give me one good reason why not!" I replied.

He got to his feet and crossed over to me.

"You're wasting a brilliant opportunity to live life, make some memories, experience new things," he explained. He pried the book from my hands and held it out of my reach. I tried to grab it, but he was too tall.

"I wasn't going to sit here the whole time. There are lots of things I can do! You know, stuff that doesn't include the sea," I snapped.

"Like?" he asked, raising an eyebrow.

"Well . . . I went exploring today. And . . . there's the spa. And swimming pools—"

"Yes, very life changing. I bet you can't do *any* of that in Florida," Ryan said sarcastically.

I narrowed my eyes at him. "I can also rent a bike and ride around the island. That's adventurous enough for me."

"Look, you're going kayaking with me, and that's that. I'm not going to let you get out of it," he said firmly.

"And what if I refuse?" I challenged, folding my arms. I should have known better than to say that.

He seized the opportunity to terrorize me within seconds, picking me up and taking me out to the balcony.

"What are you doing?" I asked frantically, trying to escape from his strong grip.

"Oh, look at that," Ryan said with an evil smile. "The sea is just a few yards below us. I wonder what would happen if I dropped you down there?"

"Are you crazy?" I cried. "What if there are rocks? What if something stings me?"

"Why don't we find out?" he asked in a low voice, his breath tickling my ear. A shiver went down my spine. He held me over the rail, ready to drop me at any second.

"No! Stop! Okay, fine, I'll go. Just don't drop me! Please!" I pleaded, clinging to him. He smirked, and let me down on the balcony. I let out a huge sigh of relief, clutching the hand railing.

"You're so cute when you panic, Aubany," he teased. I fought the urge to slap him.

"You're going to shut up and leave me alone now," I said darkly, glaring daggers at Ryan.

"Then it's settled," he sang, looking pleased with himself. He headed back inside, leaving me to wonder what I ever did to land myself in hell with the devil himself.

CHAPTER SIX

THE VOYAGE OF THE KAYAK

My first night sharing a room with Ryan was just as bad as I'd imagined. The creepy sensation of having my mortal enemy so close by kept me up until ungodly hours of the morning. I tossed and turned, unable to sleep, as I thought of all the terrible things that might happen when I went kayaking. I created so many bad scenarios that I lost count.

My plan was to wake up early the next morning and escape before he could drag me anywhere. At the crack of dawn, when it was barely light, I got up and tiptoed towards the door. Unfortunately, Ryan had anticipated my escape plans, leaving a chaotic mess of shoes and suitcases near the door to alert him if I tried to make a break for it. Unable to see my way around, I tripped on them and let out a startled yelp as I smacked into the door.

A light switched on near Ryan's bed. I rubbed my head and glanced over my shoulder. Ryan was smirking.

"Morning," he greeted. He ignored my angry expression as he added, "Trying to escape, were we?"

"I still could, you know," I replied, my hand flying to the handle.

"And I could still throw you over the balcony," he replied. "Besides, you might want to rethink your outfit before venturing outside."

I looked down at my Snoopy shirt and heart-splattered shorts that had *Hot Stuff* written across my butt and blushed furiously. *Why* had I grabbed these, of *all* the pajamas in my closet?

I grabbed a pair of shorts and a T-shirt before heading into the bathroom and slamming the door. My next plan was to stall him, so I took the longest shower I could. I washed my hair twice and myself three times, then shaved my legs, then counted to 100.

Eventually I faced the grim fact that I was wasting water and reluctantly got out.

When I emerged from the bathroom, I saw that Ryan had made himself coffee. I was on my way to pour some for myself when he handed me a steaming mug.

"You were taking ages so I already made you one," he said, looking annoyed. I was shocked.

"Um, thanks," I replied, gingerly taking it from him. I inspected it, frowning. "Did you put something in it?"

He raised an eyebrow. "Oh yeah. Filled it with dirt from the garden outside," he said, sarcastically.

"Well, you can't blame me for not trusting you," I said defensively, taking a careful sip. It tasted fine. I glanced at him again, watching as he gathered his clothes to go shower.

"How did you know I drank coffee?" I asked, truly curious.

"Because I see you drinking it from my window when you read outside on Sunday mornings," he replied, before heading into the bathroom. I frowned. Why would he be watching me?

"What if it was tea?" I challenged through the door.

"Nice try," he called back. "You drink your tea black, and your coffee with milk."

The shower water turned on after that.

I tried to ignore just how creepy that sounded and shrugged it off, turning away from the door. I mean, how was I supposed to take that? He was watching me from his window? I know he liked to annoy me, but that was just a whole new level of creepy.

~

After Ryan had hastily showered (thanks to me having taken so long), we headed over to breakfast. I stuck with something simple—cereal. My stomach had already started to churn again, and I was afraid it might violently protest if I tried to eat too much.

Ryan helped himself to toast and bacon and eggs. I should have eaten faster and escaped while he was busy making his plate. Or even skipped breakfast altogether. But, by the time the idea occurred to me, he'd already taken a seat.

Angry with myself, I ate my cereal in gloomy silence. Then I realised I could still escape while he was eating. I quickly jumped up to leave, when he grabbed my wrist. "Hold on," he said.

"Ryan, let go of me," I told him. "I'm just taking my bowl back."

"No, you're trying to run away. Give it up, Aubany," he said.

He didn't let go of my wrist, and I slumped back into my seat, defeated. I watched other people having breakfast while Ryan ate. He was eating one-handed, refusing to let go of my wrist.

Just when things were looking grim, I spotted Savannah nearby. My guardian angel! Maybe she could get me out of this!

"Savannah!" I called, waving to her. She saw me and came hurrying over.

"Hi, Aubany," she said cheerfully. Then her eye caught Ryan. "Hi there," she purred. He nodded at her and continued eating.

"I'm Savannah," she added, offering her hand.

"Ryan," he replied between mouthfuls of toast, completely oblivious to her flirting. He didn't even bother to shake her hand.

I gave Savannah an annoyed look. "Savannah, he's going to force me to go kayaking with him. Help me!" I pleaded, tugging on her wrist.

"Kayaking? Ooh, I've always wanted to try that! Can I join in?" she asked.

"What?" I exclaimed. "No, you're supposed to be getting me out of this, not encouraging him!" I groaned.

"Oh, Aubany, don't worry. You won't be touching the sea. It'll be just like the boat," she promised, pulling up a chair.

Oh, *yay*! Just like the boat? That made everything *so* much better . . .

"Listen to Savannah," Ryan said. He'd finished his breakfast.

I glared at both of them and said, "You guys suck."

"How about this," she said suddenly. "if you do it, I'll take you to the spa for a facial and massage afterward, and I'll pay for it all."

"Really?" I asked, convinced for a second. That sounded nice. Then I snapped back to reality. "No," I said firmly.

"You might as well, you're not getting out of it," Ryan told me.

"I agree," Savannah said. I think she was just trying to suck up to Ryan. I considered their words and realized how slim my chances were of escaping at that point. It pained me to admit it, but I was trapped.

"Okay, fine, I give up," I sighed. "I'll do it."

Ryan and Savannah high fived, which made me sigh in despair.

~

Sea Spray Beach was very crowded that morning. I cinched my life jacket as tightly as it would go. Ryan was pulling a kayak out of the pile as Savannah grabbed one as well.

There was *no way* I was going on my own.

"I'm with Savannah," I announced. I began to make my way over to her, when Ryan grabbed my arm.

"I don't think so. You're with me," he said, smirking.

"Why? Isn't it bad enough that you're making me do this?" I asked wearily.

"The whole point of making you do this is so I can watch you freak out. Therefore, you're coming with me."

He pulled me toward his kayak and shoved me into the front before I could get away. The waves were rushing towards me, and just watching them made me feel sick. Suddenly Ryan pushed the kayak out into the water and jumped into the back.

The waves made the kayak rock up and down. Gasping, I clung to its sides, terrified.

Ryan was already laughing. "You act like it's going to kill you!" he said.

I whimpered.

He handed me a paddle and instructed me to help. I weakly attempted to steer the kayak, but I wasn't strong enough. As a result of this, it just went in circles. After a while, Ryan noticed that and sighed.

"Man, you really are weak," he laughed. "Scared of the ocean, can't paddle a kayak . . . do you actually have any good qualities?"

I gawked at him as anger flared in me. I was thoroughly insulted by his comment.

"So you want to play it like that, huh?" I asked. "First you drag me onto this freaking kayak, out into the middle of the sea, and then you have the nerve to insult me to my face?"

"Oh, and I forgot one: you have a temper to match your flaming red hair. Did I miss anything else?" he asked slyly.

I flicked my paddle and got him square in the face with a splash of salt water. He gasped in shock. Then I freaked out, realizing I'd gotten water in the boat.

"Oh, my God!" I shouted. "Are we going to sink?"

Ryan raised an eyebrow at me as he smoothed his damp hair out of his eyes. "Are you serious?" Ryan splashed me with his paddle and soaked my shirt. I gasped, shivering. The water was freezing, and it made me smell like salt.

"Okay, we've been on a kayak. Take me back right now!" I cried.

"No way, we just got out here," he said. He paddled farther out to sea.

"Ryan . . ." I pleaded. "If we don't go back, I'm going to be sick. I swear I will."

I tried to paddle back but it just made us go in circles again. Ryan shot me an annoyed look, causing me to stop and sit rigidly in the boat. A big wave made the kayak tip drastically to one side.

"Oh, God," I muttered, clinging onto the sides of the boat. After suffering through a few more waves like that, I was feeling sick to my stomach. I was even shaking.

"Are you really that uncomfortable?" he asked me, looking surprised. I could only muster a nod.

He sighed. "Okay, fine, I'll take you in," he said, rolling his eyes. He began to paddle to the beach. As we got closer, the waves roughly pushed us toward the shore. Just a little bit farther and I'd be off the dreaded contraption.

When we finally pulled up to the shore, Ryan carefully stepped out. He glanced at me and said, "Okay, I'd get out now."

"That's the general idea," I muttered. I was almost out when I caught my foot under the seat and twisted my ankle.

"Aubany!" Ryan said urgently. I was trying to get my foot free but I couldn't. I didn't understand why he was rushing me, and I assumed he was just being annoying.

"You're so impatient," I said to him. Then I heard something behind me. I turned to see a massive wave coming straight at me. My eyes got huge.

My foot finally jerked free, but not fast enough. The wave crashed on top of me, completely flipped the kayak, and knocked me over. I went flying into the hot sand, which was covered in hard, pointy shells.

I opened my eyes, feeling something hard under my arm and something around my waist. I looked down to see another arm. I sat up and realized that Ryan had his arms around me.

He had tried to break my fall.

All I could do was blink and stare at him. I hadn't expected to crash like that, having never been kayaking in the sea before. No one had warned me that the wave wouldn't go under the kayak like it did in the middle of the sea.

"Are you okay?" Ryan asked, letting go of me quickly. He got to his feet.

"Yeah," I replied. I grabbed my paddle, which was lying nearby.

Why had Ryan tried to stop my fall? It would have been so much more amusing to watch me go flying into the sand.

His blue eyes were wide open with what I swear might have been concern, and his hair was soaked and dripping from the wave. His gaze dropped to my arm.

"You know you're bleeding," he told me softly.

"I am?" I asked, surprised. I looked down and spotted a scratch on my arm, probably from a shell. "Oh, that's nothing," I told him, rubbing the blood away. I stood up, and Ryan pulled the kayak away from the water. "Hey . . ." I said. I wanted to thank him for saving me, but before I got a chance, he turned to me and grinned.

"That was the funniest thing I've ever seen," he said, laughing.

I felt like I'd been stabbed in the chest. One moment he'd been concerned, the next he was back to his usual self. I gave him a bitter look.

"Oh, forget it," I grumbled. I turned away from him, folding my arms.

"Aubany!" a voice shouted. I looked over to see Savannah flying across the beach towards me. "Are you all right?" she asked, looking worried.

I smiled at her. "Fine. I survived, so I'm fine."

"See? It wasn't such a big deal," came Ryan's voice from behind me. He was awfully close. I turned and felt his hand graze mine. I looked down and realized he was taking my paddle from me.

"I need your life jacket, too," he replied. I handed it over and he headed off.

That had been strange. The Ryan I knew would have made me take my own paddle back. And he definitely wouldn't have tried to save me.

~

I returned to my room that night after spending the afternoon with Savannah at the pool. She'd made good on her promise, and our glowing spa treatments had left us feeling relaxed and girly—the perfect frame of mind for lounging around the pool and checking out cute guys.

I was pretty tired, which wasn't surprising considering my traumatic ordeal with the kayak, so I went straight to bed. The sheets still weren't familiar to me, so I had a hard time getting comfortable.

Ryan was out, which was a relief. I didn't really care where he'd gone or what he was doing. I shut my eyes and tried to imagine that I was home in my own bed. It didn't really work, but I felt myself slowly drifting off to sleep regardless.

That was, until I felt something move in my bed.

CHAPTER SEVEN

THE DEFINITION OF HATE

My eyes shot open. Something *slimy* was moving up my leg! I ripped back the covers, revealing a cluster of worms. I screamed and jumped out of the bed.

God, *gross!*

I grabbed one of my least favourite shirts and scooped them up, wiped the sheets clean, then let them loose in the garden and went back inside. I took a quick shower to wash off the horrible, slimy sensation I'd felt.

What had they been doing in my bed? I was willing to bet Ryan had something to do with it. It was exactly the jerk-ass kind of thing he would do.

Not surprisingly, I couldn't sleep after that, so once I'd checked both beds and the rest of the room for any more creatures, I turned on the TV and tried to find something to take my mind off the worms.

Not long after, Ryan came in. He took one look at me and then went into the bathroom. I turned off the TV and lay there, trying to go to sleep. A few moments later, he came back out and got into his own bed. I snuck a glance at him, but he was just lying there.

Waiting, no doubt.

"If you're waiting for the worms, they're gone," I said finally, looking at him.

"It is? You found them?" he asked.

"So it *was* you!" I declared, sitting up. "That wasn't funny, it was just plain gross!"

He started laughing, like he didn't consider it gross at all. "How did you react?" he asked.

I gave him a *duh* look and said, "How do you *think* I reacted?"

"I should have set up a camera. I didn't think you'd get back before me," he said. I rolled my eyes.

"Good*night*, Ryan," I said, before rolling over and shutting my eyes.

I lied there for a while, missing my home, and my parents. I wondered how Mom was doing, all the way in California. My thoughts wandered to other subjects, like the traumatic kayaking experience. Ryan had said it was a good thing; that he was helping me face my fear of the ocean. But the only good thing that had come out of it was the way his arms had wrapped around me when I fell . . .

Wait, what?

I frowned. That was *not* something I should have thought. Ryan was a jerk, a fact I knew all too well. Somehow, I still couldn't figure out why he'd done it.

"Hey . . . Ryan," I called out softly.

There was a tiny groan. "What?"

I hesitated. What if my question sounded weird?

"*What?*" he asked again, sounding irritated.

"Um . . . well," I began, "why did you try to catch me when I fell out of the kayak?"

There was a small silence. "I didn't," he replied finally. "You fell into me."

I went red. I was glad he couldn't see that in the darkness.

"Oh," I replied. Of course I fell into him! Why would Ryan try to break my fall? I scolded myself for thinking such a stupid idea. Ryan was nothing but a jerk, and that was all he'd ever be, so I needed to banish any crazy thoughts of him turning into a romantic, immediately.

~

The next morning, I slept in. By the time I woke up, Ryan had left, and I was on my own to do what I wanted for the day. I could have kissed the Fates. Freedom! I planned to make the most of it.

I had a more substantial breakfast, with the comforting knowledge that I wasn't going to chuck it all up. I filled my plate with crispy bacon, buttery toast and fried eggs. Delicious!

After that, I went to Reception to check out the tours. There were quite a few to choose from, but they all sounded too adventurous. Helicopter tours, seaplane tours, tours around the islands and through the rainforest too. Eventually, I settled for the rainforest one because it didn't involve boarding any boats to other islands.

The tour was long and . . . well, not all that exciting. It was pretty, and I got to hear birds chirping and water running, but it wasn't anything spectacular. There were some keen photographers on the tour though, who kept snapping pictures of birds and exotic plants, so I guess it couldn't have been *that* bad. Maybe it was just me.

When I got back to the room I was out of things to do. I could go swimming . . . again. Or go shopping and blow all my money. But it all seemed pretty boring and plain. I hated to admit it, but I felt like I was missing out.

It was funny, but I kind of wished Ryan was here making me do activities. But, after yesterday's episode, I doubted he'd try it again. Ryan was probably off enjoying himself, and I wished I had the strength to join him. I hated the ocean, but he did have a point when he said I couldn't sit here for six weeks doing nothing—and a bigger one when he said I needed to face my fears.

I realized, after a little while, that this was the perfect opportunity to give my Mom a call and see how she was doing. I dialled her number and waited.

"Hello," answered a voice which sounded like my Dad.

"Hi Dad, it's Aubany," I replied. "How are you?"

"Aubany! I'm good! Were you after Mom?" he asked.

"Yeah," I replied.

"I'm sorry Aubany . . . she's not available right now. She's in the middle of a session with the doctor."

"Oh . . ." I trailed off. I'd sort of been hoping I could talk to her about Ryan's behaviour, and I didn't usually share that kind of stuff with Dad. It was something Mom understood better. Plus, I still wasn't comfortable enough with the idea of Mom in treatment to be openly discussing that either. But I wanted to be supportive, and I *was* concerned as to whether she was all right.

"Well, how's it going?" I swallowed hard, trying to keep it together.

"It's going well, actually. The doctor says it's too early to say if it's working, but she's been handling it well so far."

"Oh . . . that's good then," I said, meaning it. "What . . . what kind of treatment is it?"

"Hormone therapy," he replied. "Yeah . . . so it's . . . it's intense. They're discussing removing some of her glands to control the cancer growth."

"Oh, my God," I blurted out, getting a bad visual of Mom being sliced open. "Oh . . . my *God* . . ."

"Sorry, I didn't mean to alarm you," he said, sounding apologetic. "Don't you stress too much about it—your mom's a tough woman. She'll get through it."

"I . . ." I trailed off, clutching the phone tightly. This was exactly why I *hadn't* want to come to terms with it. I knew cancer was deadly, and the fact that they had to do such serious *procedures* . . .

"Are you all right, Aubany? Tell you what, let's talk about you, alright? What's happening on the island?"

I quickly recovered, glad to have a subject change. "Uh, it's fine. Yeah. It's . . ." I trailed off, not quite sure how to describe it. I mean, it wasn't like I was having a blast, but I wasn't *miserable*. I was just . . . *bored*, I guess.

"You know, it's not bad," I said finally. "I just can't do much because of my fear of the ocean, and *Ryan* hasn't been much help but . . . well, I'm getting through it."

"That's good," he replied. "Oh, it looks like your mother's coming out now. I'd better go. But stay positive, Aubany. You'll be fine."

"Thanks Dad," I said, smiling. I felt better after hearing his voice.

"I love you," he said.

"I love you, too," I replied, before bidding him goodbye and hanging up. I exhaled slowly, before getting up to switch on the TV.

When Ryan finally returned in the late afternoon, I was curled up on the bed watching a movie. He walked over to the counter and leaned against it, taking in the scene of me lying comfortably on the bed.

"Did you even go out today?" he asked, eyeing me.

"Yes. I went on the rainforest tour," I replied.

"Wow. I didn't think you had the courage to go near anything related to nature," he said, smirking.

Okay, I take it all back— the wishful thinking that Ryan would whisk me off to more activities. I'd rather sulk alone than be insulted by a jerk all day.

"Well, what did *you* do?" I asked, wanting to steer the conversation away from another fight. He dumped his backpack down on the countertop and flashed me a grin.

"I went kite surfing. It was so much fun . . . not that you'd understand," he said. "You know, Aubany, I *do* feel sorry for you. Your fear of the ocean is a real obstacle when it comes to having a good time."

I bit back a bad-mouthed retort. "Well, congratulations. You did something *extraordinary*," I said bitterly.

He slumped down on his bed, looking exhausted.

"So, what do you plan on doing tomorrow?" I asked point blank.

"I thought I'd go diving," he replied. My insides felt like they'd flopped inside out. *Diving*? Under the sea? With all the sea creatures, and the sharks and jellyfish? That sounded like the most unappealing idea ever.

But so did another day of just lying around watching TV.

Suddenly, the idea was . . . tempting.

Maybe it was my inner thrill seeker revealing itself. (Not that I even knew I had that side to me.) But, all of a sudden, I really wanted to try diving. The idea was terrifying, yes, but it was also different. And maybe Ryan was right. Maybe this *would* be good for me.

"Can I come with you?" I asked quietly.

Ryan stared at me in shock. "What?"

My eyes widened as I realized what a stupid question that was. We *hated* each other. The last thing he wanted was me tagging along just so I could freak out with the fishes. Hell, his very presence annoyed me, so why would I willingly hang out with him? What the heck was I thinking?

"Really?" he asked, sounding surprised. "You want to go diving?"

"No, I changed my mind," I said quickly. "Diving? Underwater? No way. I'm just gonna stay here."

I turned away from him and busied myself with my books, arranging them in order.

"Aubany," I heard him say, "you can come diving, if you want. I don't mind."

I looked over to him. He looked almost hopeful.

"But I'll just freak out," I said. "Besides, you don't want me hanging around. You're supposed to hate me, remember?" I said.

I stood up and walked out to the balcony, shutting the door behind me. The salty air made me queasy again, but it was better than the tense air inside. I heard the door slide open. Ryan appeared at my side.

"Who said anything about hating you?" he asked. "I don't hate you," he added firmly.

I raised an eyebrow at him and burst out laughing. "Oh, yeah? Wow, that's a good one," I said.

He frowned. "I don't," he insisted.

"You make my life a living hell. You insult me, you tease me, and you pull pranks on me! And now you're saying you *don't* hate me? God, how much of a jerk can you be?" I snapped angrily.

Ryan looked shocked. I pushed away from him and stormed back inside, crossed the room, and headed out the front door.

I took a long walk to clear my head, not wanting to think about Ryan or diving or *anything* related to the ocean, all of which was pretty hard to do while stuck on a goddamn freaking island!

~

I ran into Savannah as I was making my way past the pools. She had a towel around her waist and was wearing a damp bikini.

"Hey!" she greeted me brightly. Her enthusiasm was like a ray of sunshine.

"Hi," I replied.

She noticed my sour mood. "Everything okay?" she asked.

I shrugged. "I guess," I sighed.

She glanced over her shoulder, then grabbed my arm and said, "Come with me. I found something cool this morning."

I followed her as she led me around the pools and down a secluded, pebbled path.

We rounded a bend and found a small beach, hidden away from the rest of the island by a large, rocky cliff and a few palm trees. It was the perfect spot for two lovers. It even had a hammock.

I *loved* hammocks. There was just something appealing about hanging in midair. Whenever I spotted a hammock, I always had a tendency to run to it . . . which is exactly what I did. Savannah followed behind.

"A hammock!" I cried out, as I launched myself onto it. Or at least, I attempted to. As it turns out, the Fates were having their way with me again, and this hammock wasn't planning on bonding with me anytime soon.

Instead of landing on the hammock, I somehow managed to launch myself over it. I landed with a thud on my back in the sand. A shot of pain went up my spine.

"Ow . . ." I groaned, sitting up. I rubbed my aching back. Then, for some reason I couldn't stop laughing. How the heck had I managed that? Then, I heard even more laughter. Savannah was cracking up, leaning against the palm tree for support.

"That was hilarious; you just went flying over it. Your face when you hit the ground . . . priceless," she said. I gave her a mock-annoyed look. "I thought you brought me here to cheer me up, not cause me more suffering!" I said between my giggles. I pushed myself up off the sand and cautiously seated myself onto the hammock, then laid down. My back still hurt from the impact. Savannah climbed on at the opposite end, so we were both lying side by side, swinging, watching the palm trees sway over our heads and listening to the ocean waves.

"Do you want to talk about it?" she asked me finally. I found myself rather comfortable being around Savannah, almost like I'd known her my entire life, and I decided if I was going to tell anyone it may as well be her.

"It's nothing, really. Ryan was just being a jerk, as usual," I replied.

Savannah was silent for a few moments.

"If Ryan hates you so much, why does he make you hang out with him?" she asked suddenly.

"It's because he likes to annoy me," I replied.

"In my experience, guys who annoy you usually end up liking you," she said openly.

I sat up, staring at her in shock. "You've got to be kidding me!" I exclaimed, disbelievingly. "We've known each other since we were kids! He hates me. You should have seen how mad he was this one time when I destroyed one of his Lego houses. Not to mention all the mean things he's done to me."

"Destroying his Lego house? No *wonder* he hates you," Savannah teased. "If you'd done that to me, I'd be holding a grudge too!"

"Oh, shut up," I said lightly. I'd had a perfectly good reason to destroy it. He and one of his friends had been teasing me, and I'd stumbled upon the creation as I was running off to find a hiding spot. He'd been asking for it.

Savannah and I chatted for a while, which successfully took my mind off the fight from earlier with Ryan. I didn't even realize until I'd begun to head back to the room that the sound of the waves hadn't made me feel queasy at all. That was unusual, considering they usually did.

I stopped in my tracks, only halfway across Sea Spray Beach, and wandered over to the water.

Cautiously, I stuck my toes in it. It was cold . . . and harmless. Just like a swimming pool.

I decided that the ocean was strange. It had a whole other world hidden beneath its waters, full of both danger and beauty. It was an adventure all its own, like a jungle or a snowy mountain. But I guessed the most beautiful things were hidden where only the most daring could find them. Beauty like that was only for those who had the courage to earn it.

I don't know whether it was the appeal of the island inviting me to uncover its secrets, pure boredom driving me to madness, or even a deeper feeling that wanted to prove to Ryan that I wasn't a terrified, weak kid, but, at that moment, I decided to take the plunge into my deepest fears, and face the very thing that stood in the way of me truly enjoying this vacation.

I waded a little way into the ocean and stood on the wet, sandy shoreline, with waves rushing past my knees. I stood there, daring myself to go further. The dimly lit sky made it seem all the more terrifying. I couldn't see what might be lurking under the waves. But I felt a tiny thrill run through me. The smell of the sea salt was both sickening and intoxicating.

I felt more alive than I ever had before.

I couldn't even begin to understand where my courage had suddenly sprouted from, or why I was so determined to fight my fear. I guess once I got a taste of the madness, I wanted more of it. I didn't want to sit around and let Ryan taunt me for six weeks. I was going to show him what I was really made of.

Scared of the ocean, can't paddle a kayak . . . do you actually have any good qualities?

The memory stung my heart. He wanted good qualities? I'd give him good qualities. Starting with my determination to send that smug, stuck-up attitude right back where it came from.

CHAPTER EIGHT

THRILL SEEKING

By the time I got back to the room, all the thoughts in my head had changed from when I left. There was no longer anger directed at Ryan, just pure determination to prove him wrong. I had a new approach.

He was waiting for me when I returned.

"I'm sorry," was the first thing he said.

I didn't believe it, but I replied with, "Apology accepted."

His eyes lit up a little. "So . . . does that mean you're not angry anymore?"

I flashed him a sweet smile, which completely put him off guard, and said, "Angry? Why no, I'm perfectly fine with your teasing and taunting. Which is why I will, in fact, be going diving with you to-morrow."

He looked completely confused. "So . . . you *are* still angry," he said.

I sighed, the charade wearing off.

"No, I'm not angry with you, Ryan. I'm just trying really hard not to cause another fight here."

He then noticed my legs, still wet from my venture into the sea.

"Did you go swimming or something?" he asked.

"Something like that. It was nice," I said, and I headed to the bathroom to grab a towel. I began drying off my legs.

"Like, in a pool?" he asked.

"No, the ocean," I replied, trying to hide my smug smile.

"Are you joking, Aubany?" he asked, looking shocked. "Because you're starting to creep me out."

Ha! The tables had certainly turned now! Score one for Team Aubany!

I hung up the towel and crossed over to him. I lightly patted his shoulder and smiled.

"Don't look so freaked out. I'm just embracing my inner thrill seeker," I said.

He narrowed his eyes. "You? A *thrill seeker*? Yeah, right. After what I saw yesterday the only thing you could possibly get a thrill out of is a comfy lounge chair." Sadly enough, the idea of a comfy lounge chair did sound quite enticing. But I wasn't about to tell him that.

"Well, maybe you don't know me well enough to understand all the different sides to me," I said. "After all, the closest thing you've ever done in terms of trying to get to know me is pull pranks. And, since all they do is make me upset, I guess you've never gotten a very appealing picture of me, have you?"

He frowned. "I don't pull pranks to annoy you," he said.

I let out a laugh. "Could have fooled me," I said bitterly, before heading over to the menu that was on the fridge. "Are we eating out tonight or ordering in?"

"Oh, I don't know. Which one would *appeal* to you most?" Ryan asked, his snarky tone returning.

I began to feel the need to win this argument. I imagined that eating in would make me look like I wanted to enjoy a 'comfy life', so I chose eating out. "There's a restaurant over on Tarang Island," I said, glaring. "Why don't we take a little boat ride?"

"Fine then, Little Miss *Thill Seeker*. We'll take a boat ride and see how long it takes for you to chuck up your dinner."

We left the room, bickering the whole way to the docks. The boats were kind of like taxis, little dinghies that were operated by hotel staff. We got into one and I focused on acting normally, resisting the urge to cling to the sides of the boat. When we started moving, I pretended we were in a car, riding over rocky roads and not bumpy waves.

Ryan was watching me with an amused expression.

"You're still tense," he noted.

"No, I'm not," I protested.

"Oh, really?" he asked, leaning in closer. I felt something brush against my leg and let out a squeal that startled the boat driver. It had just been Ryan's leg. He smirked at me.

"Told you. Oh, Aubany, did you really think you could fool me? Thrill seeking? Swims in the ocean?" He narrowed his eyes at me. "I don't believe a word of it. I'd even bet money that, when we step off this boat, you're going to be sick."

I would have challenged him, but I feared he might be right, and I knew better than to let his stupid taunting get the better of me – and my wallet.

When we arrived on the island, we headed along a path towards the restaurant. The building was painted in bright colours—sunny yellow, mint green, peachy pink. We walked in and got a table together. Never, in all my years, did I ever see myself sitting at a table—in a *restaurant*—with Ryan Rupert. It was almost like a date.

The thought made me cringe.

I wasn't feeling all that well, just as Ryan had suspected. But I hadn't vomited yet, which was a good sign. I forced myself to take deep breaths, and focused on the lines in the wood of the table.

"So, you actually want to go diving tomorrow?" Ryan asked, looking skeptical. He folded his arms and leaned back in his chair, raising an eyebrow.

"Yes," I replied. "It'll be fun."

He shot me an amused look. "Right. Because I can totally see you swimming in the sea and considering it 'fun,'" he said.

The waitress brought us a bottle of water and two glasses. She gave Ryan a smile and her eyes lingered on him for a second or two.

"Can I pour it for you?" she offered.

I rolled my eyes. I hardly thought it was necessary. I was pretty sure we were both capable of pouring our own water. But I didn't say anything as Ryan leaned back and said, "Go ahead."

She filled both our glasses and asked if we were ready to order. We told her we'd be ready in a few minutes and she headed off.

Ryan smirked and said, "Girls. Can't keep their eyes off me."

I let out a laugh. "Right. Because you're *so* good looking," I said.

"Well your new friend certainly seems to think so," Ryan stated, referring to Savannah. "And didn't you just admit it?"

"I was being sarcastic," I replied, avoiding his gaze.

"Ah, but we both know that's a lie," he said slowly.

"Are you *always* this full of yourself?" I asked, folding my arms. "No wait, I don't even have to ask because I know you are. It's one of the many down-falls of being your neighbour."

"Oh?" he said. "And what would be the perks?"

"It's funny, I can't seem to think of any," I drawled, opening my menu to find something worth ordering.

"Surely there has to be something," he said.

I ignored him, and I could sense his frustration. Suddenly, he snatched the menu out of my hands, just as the waitress came back. I gawked, but before I could say anything—

"So, are you ready to order?" the waitress asked.

"We'll both have the lobster special," Ryan said.

I was at a loss for words, unable to form a coherent sentence as she wrote it down. She said it wouldn't be long, then walked off. I glared at Ryan. "Why did you order for me?" I growled.

"Well, that's one of my good qualities," he replied. "You didn't have to bother."

I couldn't *believe* he'd done that. I leaned back in my seat, only to wince in pain as I hit the spot where I'd fallen earlier. As I shot forward in my seat, Ryan narrowed his eyes at me.

"What's up with your back?" he asked. "Did you hurt it in the kayak yesterday?"

"No, I fell trying to get into a hammock," I snapped.

He stared at me for a few moments.

Then he burst out laughing.

"Are you serious?" he asked. "Wow, Aubany. I can *so* see you as a thrill seeker. Terrified of the ocean, can't steer a kayak, can't even get into a hammock—"

I cut him off. "Stop right there," I hissed. "Not another word."

"But it's true," he pointed out. He studied my expression. "Wait," he said. "*That's* what this is about, isn't it?"

I was silent, fuming.

"Oh, Aubany, I didn't realise it annoyed you so much. If only I'd known that a few simple words were enough to get under your skin, I wouldn't have bothered pulling pranks all the time," he said.

P.S.Malcolm

"How can you say you don't hate me when you say stuff like that?" I snapped.

"Hey," he said. "I'm just pointing out the facts."

"Well, can you not? Everyone has flaws," I said. Speaking of flaws, I wished I could find out a few of his. It would be nice to have something to hold over him every time he brought up one of mine.

"You're right," he sighed. "I shouldn't tease the less fortunate."

I gritted my teeth.

Luckily, our dinner arrived before I could lose my cool. I had to admit, it smelled pretty good. But, as I ate, the churning in my stomach intensified. I suddenly felt like eating had been a very bad idea, and I still needed to get back to the main island after dinner.

I tried to take another bite, but my stomach wasn't having it. I jumped up and raced to the bathroom.

I can't say vomiting in a restaurant bathroom toilet was my proudest moment. It certainly wasn't something I ever saw myself doing. When I'd finished, and the sick feeling had gone from my stomach, I went to the sink to wash my face. I still had that horrible bitter taste in my mouth, and I felt light-headed.

As I walked out of the bathroom, I saw Ryan waiting for me outside. He turned to me with a smirk and said,

"Told you."

~

The rest of the evening passed painfully slow. Ryan was smug because he'd been right about me vomiting, and I didn't have the stomach to eat much more of my lobster special afterwards. The ride back was just as bad as the one there, but, luckily, I didn't feel the need to get sick again after.

I was angry and tired, so, when we got back to the room, I changed in the bathroom and went straight to bed without looking at or talking to Ryan. He seemed to notice my defeated mood, but thankfully he must've also decided that he'd bullied me enough for the night, and he didn't take advantage of it.

When morning came, I was rudely awakened by the curtains being parted, which allowed the harsh sunlight to burn behind my eyelids. I groaned and blinked, turning over to bury my face in my pillow. But the pillow was whipped away from me, followed by the blankets.

"Come on, *thrill seeker*," Ryan's smug voice sounded. "Don't want to be late for our little underwater exploration, do we?"

I'd forgotten about my decision to go diving, and was already starting to regret it.

"I've changed my mind again," I muttered.

"Oh, *no*, you haven't," Ryan said. He grabbed my arms and pulled me out of bed. "Off you go. Change, shower, all of that. Maybe try and keep it under forty minutes this time," he said.

I shot him an annoyed look as I gathered some clothes and headed for the bathroom.

"Don't suppose I can count on you making me a coffee again?" I asked.

"We'll see," he said, giving me a glance. It had been a joke, but his comment changed that. I pushed it to the back of my mind and shut the door, then proceeded to shower.

When I came out twenty minutes later, I noticed that Ryan had two cups of coffee on the counter. Without a word, I passed him and took the one that hadn't been touched. It felt weird, having him make me coffee.

"Not going to thank me?" he asked from the bed.

"Thank you," I said quickly, not wanting to linger on the subject. A part of me wondered if he really *did* put something in it this time.

"We'll leave in ten minutes," he decided, before heading to the bathroom. This whole charade was starting to feel like a routine. It was unnerving, having an actual *routine* with my mortal enemy.

I drank my coffee, which again tasted fine, and checked my phone for any messages. I hadn't had

126

any updates from my parents since I'd last called them. Just thinking about what Mom was going through gave me confidence. If *she* could undergo hormone therapy, then *surely* I could go diving. Compared to what Mom had to endure, my problem wasn't nearly *half* as bad! I kept that in mind as I mentally prepared myself for the day ahead.

~

A short while later Ryan and I found ourselves down at the docks with a bunch of other people, waiting to board a boat that would take us out to the diving spot. Now my insides were beginning to churn. I was nervous. Why had I gone and put myself in a situation like this?

I could turn around now. Walk away. It would mean I'd lose the battle against Ryan about proving to him that I could face my fears. It would mean letting myself down. But I'd be safe, and probably happier than I would be in a few moments when I was on that boat.

Ryan gripped my wrist as we began to board, like he was afraid I'd run off. I followed him silently, knowing better now than to try and fight his death grip. He was too strong, and I'd probably only end up twisting my arm and causing another injury.

When we were on board, the panic finally settled in. I suddenly realised that I was going underwater, to the very place where my fears originated. And all because of what? A stupid, courageous moment on the beach that had been so fleeting I wondered if it had even meant anything at all? A chance to prove to the guy I hated that I wasn't weak?

I was a complete idiot.

"I can't do this," I said finally. There was still time to get off. I headed for the exit, but Ryan grabbed me.

"Come on, didn't you say it would be fun?" Ryan teased.

"I wasn't thinking straight," I said quickly. "You win, okay? I'm weak. I can't do anything right. And

I'll never get over my fear of the ocean. You can tease me all you like. Just let me get off!"

His expression suddenly turned serious. "No," Ryan said. "I won't let you."

"Ryan, *please*," I said.

He shook his head.

The boat started up and moved away from the docks.

Great.

"Listen to me," Ryan said softly. "I know you can face your fear of the ocean. You need someone to help you, someone to force you to do what I know you're capable of doing. And you already hate my guts, so I'm the perfect person, right?"

I gawked at him.

"You want to *help* me?" I asked, utterly confused.

"You do have one good quality, Aubany," he said. "You're quite determined, which I hadn't noticed before. You try so hard to win your arguments against me, to have the last word, and to prove to me that my constant pranks aren't worth your tears. You wanted

129

to prove to me last night that you were game enough to cross the ocean on a boat. You still vomited, but it didn't stop you from doing it. Twice, I might add."

All I could do was stare at him as he talked.

"And now, you're going to dive into those watery depths, and you're going to realise that the ocean is not as scary as you make it out to be. And you're going to be fine, because I'm here with you. Okay?"

Dumbfounded, all I could manage was a small nod. The last thing I'd been expecting was for him to be *kind* to me. I couldn't decipher why he'd *want* to be—what was in it for *him*? I sat down on a seat and waited until we were parked out in the middle of the diving spot.

My mind was racing, creating all sorts of worst-case scenarios in my head. But I stopped myself, remembering my thoughts from this morning—it was just *swimming*. It wasn't like I was getting sliced open to remove cancer from my body. What I was about to do wouldn't *kill* me.

Well . . . at least, I *hoped* it wouldn't.

The instructor was teaching those of us who had no clue how to dive. I listened to most of what he said. He showed us how we'd put on the gear, and enter the water, and told us we'd get a chance to practise before we all went under as a group. Then we put on our diving suits and got ready to jump in.

Ryan jumped in without hesitation, landing with a small splash. He resurfaced and looked up at me.

"Come on," he said, reaching out and waving me into the water. I gripped the side of the boat. What was I doing?

"No way," I said, teetering.

"No, no backing out now," Ryan said. "Get in the water now, Aubany. It's no different than a swimming pool."

"It's *completely* different!" I protested. "There are *things* in the water."

"Yeah, that's why we're wearing diving suits," Ryan replied. "Nothing's going to hurt you, okay? I promise."

"You don't know that," I said, shrinking back.

He sighed. "If anything tries to bite you, I will use my snarky comments and sarcastic wit to send it off crying," he said.

I snorted. That was the most ridiculous thing I had ever heard.

I took a deep breath. Better to just get it over with. I jumped, trying not to think about what I was jumping into. I hit the water's surface and went under, bubbles tickling my skin as I sank. I quickly scrambled to the surface. When I shot out of the water, I gasped for air.

"Calm down," Ryan said quickly. I steadied myself and met his eyes.

"See? It's not that bad," he said calmly.

I could smell the ocean and taste it on my lips. It made me feel slightly sick, but that was like it had been on the shoreline. I wasn't that freaked out. I wondered if it was just the motion of the boats that caused the sickness, as opposed to being in the water itself. I mean, I hadn't really put myself in seawater before now, knowing what it would do to me—or, at least, what I'd *assumed* it would do to me. I'd avoided anything *associated* with it as a result. But a few days on the island had given me time to adjust to the salty air, so I wasn't getting the urge to throw up while floating in the waves.

"I'm right here," Ryan added.

"I know. I can *see* you," I replied.

He smirked. "Well, at least your charming retorts have returned," he said.

When everyone was in the water, and we'd done a few duck dives to test our gear and get used to the sensation of the air pressurising, the instructor finally let us go under. I really didn't want to, but I wasn't hanging around alone at the top while everyone else swam off.

Air tank secured and diving gear in place, I took a deep breath to reassure myself I *could* breathe, and I followed Ryan under the water.

My first thought was *wow*.

Seeing an underwater reef with my own eyes was nothing like seeing it on a postcard. The sunlight danced through the water in rays, casting shadows on the rocks and sea floor. Colourful coral sprouted everywhere like some kind of art sculpture display, but it was breathing life.

Fish swam past us, scaring the living daylights out of me. Ryan noticed them and looked back to see my panicked expression. He took my hand in his to reassure me, since we couldn't speak to each other under the water.

He led me deeper into the beautiful underwater paradise I'd been so scared of moments before. It was like another world down there—a world that had suddenly become very real to me. It was something hidden beneath the surface of our planet that I'd been so afraid to seek out.

Now I couldn't even remember why I'd been so scared.

I was fascinated. Drawn in. I wanted to reach out and run my fingers along the coral, but I knew doing so would damage it, so I didn't. It felt a bit like I was dreaming as I floated along, and if the water hadn't been so cold, I might not have believed any of this was real.

When it was time to resurface, we went back up. Only then did I realise I'd spent the whole time holding Ryan's hand. I let go as we reached the water's surface. We got back onto the boat and stripped off our diving gear.

As the boat headed back to the docks, I faced Ryan.

"Thank you," I said quietly. I wanted to tell him *Thank you for not giving up on me* or *Thank you for not letting me go back*. But I couldn't quite make the words come out, considering it was him I was talking to.

Still, from the look on his face, I didn't think I had to.

CHAPTER NINE

TANGO TEASING

When I got back to the room I saw that I had a missed call from Savannah. She'd called hours earlier, but seeing as a phone wasn't going to do me much good under the sea, I'd left it in the room. I called her back and waited.

"Aubany!" she exclaimed when she answered. "I found out that there's a dance thingy happening at Sea Spray Beach tonight."

"A dance thingy?" I repeated.

"There's going to be a bonfire, and there will *definitely* be boys. Say you'll come. Please?" she begged.

"Sure, why not?" I replied.

I heard a squeal of excitement on the other end. "Awesome! I'll meet you there," she said. Then she hung up.

Her phone call reminded me that I needed to call my parents, so I headed out to the balcony for some privacy and dialled my Dad.

"Hi Aubany," he answered. A feeling of home-sickness washed over me when I heard his voice. I missed my parents so much. "I was planning on call-ing you tonight actually. How is everything?" he asked.

"Well, it's as good as it's going to get," I replied dully. Then I laughed. "No, I'm being dramatic. It's not that bad."

"That's a relief. I was worried about you," he replied.

"Ryan's been a pain in the ass, but that's nothing new. I've actually braved the water a few times," I said.

"Really?" he asked. "Your mother will be glad to hear that. Should I put her on?"

"Yes, please," I said. I waited until I heard Mom's voice.

"Hello, Sweetheart," she said. We chatted for a while about the island, my going diving, meeting Savannah, and the hammock incident. I left out the kayak. It was too embarrassing.

"Well, that's good to hear," she said, sounding happy. "It sounds like you and Ryan are bonding a little."

"Bonding?" I snorted. "Mom, all we do is bicker. He's so snarky," I said.

"Well, he sounded nice enough when you told me about the diving story," she replied.

"That was different," I said. I could tell Mom didn't believe me.

"Dad told me you were undergoing *hormone therapy*?" I said, wanting to change the subject. "It sounds painful."

"Well, it's an operation, sweetheart. They put you to sleep for it," she replied.

I grimaced.

"I know that, but . . . *afterwards*. You know?"

"Well, I'd much rather lose my hormones than my life," Mom said pointedly, which seemed to wake me up a bit.

"I can't wrap my head around the seriousness of this," I said finally. "It feels like a huge dream. I'm here on this *island*—a beautiful paradise, and you're going through hell miles away from me. I can't even picture it without being there with you."

"I know it's hard, but you shouldn't *have* to picture it," she said gently. "I want you to remember me the way I always am—happy, and most importantly, *alive*."

"Mom, don't say that," I said quickly.

"No, just listen," she said. "No matter *what* happens, I want you to have only *good* memories of me. I have every intention of coming back to you, but we all know there's a possibility I might *not*, and if that happens . . . I don't want you to see me the way I am."

I felt myself tearing up.

"Don't cry," she said, hearing me sniffle. "Sweetheart, it's alright. It's going to be alright," she insisted, and I dried my eyes on my sleeve.

"Okay," I said. "I understand."

"Good girl," she said soothingly. "Sweetheart, I've got to go." She told me to stay safe. I wished her luck, then she hung up.

I took a few moments to compose myself before heading back inside. I found Ryan flipping through one of my books.

"I don't think I've ever seen you with a book in your hands," I said.

"Do you actually read this stuff?" he asked, handing it back.

"Don't judge me on my book taste. At least I have taste," I replied, putting the book back with the others.

"So what's this dance thingy I heard you talking about on the phone?" Ryan asked, changing the subject.

"It's a thing at the beach," I replied. "Apparently there's going to be a bonfire."

"Are you going to go?" he asked.

I nodded.

"Can I come?" he asked.

I raised an eyebrow.

"Why are you asking me? It's not *my* bonfire dance thingy," I said.

"I meant it as in, would you be annoyed if I went?" he said.

I frowned. "I wouldn't really care," I said finally. I crossed over to the dresser to find something suitable to wear. The only thing I'd brought that was remotely worthy of a "dance thingy" was the same white dress I'd worn to Josh's fortieth birthday party. The same one I was wearing when Ryan had pushed me into the pool.

I deliberated whether to wear it or not, then decided that I had nothing else, so I'd have to. I went to the bathroom to change. The dress had a lace trim bottom, and pearl buttons up the front. It floated around my knees lightly as a feather.

I pulled the sides of my bangs back so my hair was half up, half down, and I secured it with a white flower clip. I debated putting on makeup, then decided just a little bit would be okay. When I was done, I emerged from the bathroom.

Ryan was watching TV, but he looked up when I came out. He stared.

"You're wearing that dress again," he said, not taking his eyes off me.

"Yes, and it's a miracle it wasn't ruined the first time," I replied, before turning away from him.

"I'm sorry about that," he said quietly. "I didn't mean to . . . well, I didn't know and . . . I shouldn't have done it."

"It's in the past," I said. "No use going on about it."

"Right," he said. He cleared his throat, then went over to his side of the dresser and found some clothes. He went to the bathroom to change.

I occupied myself by reading while he was in there. I heard the shower running. A good half hour later he came out, dressed in a simple white button down shirt that looked pretty damn good on him, and black pants. His hair still glistened with a few droplets of water from the shower.

Now I was staring.

I quickly snapped out of it and returned to my book, refusing to look at him again. But I couldn't deny the fact that I wanted to.

He was a jerk, but that didn't change the fact that he was hot. And he was wearing something that kept tempting me to sneak glances.

I eventually gave in and took another peek.

He was sitting across from me on his bed, drying his hair with a towel. When he looked up, our eyes met.

I quickly snapped my gaze back down to my book and pretended to read.

I could feel him smirking at me.

"Is that blush on your cheeks I see, Aubany? And *not* the makeup kind?" he asked smugly.

I looked up again. "I have no idea what you're talking about."

"You are *so* blushing," he stated. "I told you. Girls can't keep their eyes off me. And *you* are no exception."

I narrowed my eyes at him. "All hot guys are jerks. And *you* are no exception either."

"So you admit that I'm hot," he said.

I rolled my eyes. "Yes. But don't get too excited."

"Why would I get excited?" he asked, crossing over to me. "If anything, it looks like *you're* the one getting a bit excited."

I snapped my book shut.

"You wish," I taunted. I left the book on my bed and crossed over to the mini fridge to get myself a bottle of water.

"Well. . . seeing as you're being honest, I'll be honest with you, too," he said, crossing over to me. He leaned in so his breath tickled my ear.

"You should wear that dress more often. It looks good on you," he said.

I stared at him, shocked. Coming from him, I couldn't tell if it was a compliment or another rude remark about the one time when it *hadn't* suited me all that well.

"What's that supposed to mean?" I asked finally.

"It means, as far as girls go, you're pretty hot, too," he said casually, leaning against the counter. "But don't go telling all the other girls I said that. They might get jealous." He winked.

I tried to come up with something to say, but I couldn't think of anything.

He smirked, completely aware that he'd left me speechless. "Ah, not used to compliments now, are we?" he teased softly. "It's easy enough to fight fire with fire, but when fire meets water, it just fizzles out, doesn't it?"

He hadn't moved away yet. His proximity was making it hard for me to think straight. I was backed against the counter, and he seemed to have all the words in the world to keep me there without even touching me.

"Y-you . . ." I stammered, finally remembering how words worked. "You're not serious."

"I'm very serious," he said, his eyes on mine. "Do you want to know the reason I even pushed you into that pool in the first place?"

Now I was curious. "Why?"

He reached out and ran the soft fabric trim of my dress through his hand. "It's because this dress looked so good on you, I figured I'd be able to see even *more* of you if you were soaking wet, if you know what I mean . . ."

Okay, *that* was sort of disturbing. I mean, *flattering*, but disturbing all the same. Finally, the effect of his good looks was starting to wear off and logical thinking was once again returning to me. Here I was, victim to years of his teasing and trickery, and he thought he could pull a few smooth moves and expect me to believe that he might be *interested* in me?

I pushed him away, embracing my newfound strength to defend myself against Ryan's hotness. "Nice try," I said.

I headed for the door, refusing to believe his words.

Before I left, I turned to him and added, "Stuff like that might work on most girls, but it'll take a lot more than a cheesy pick-up line to fool me."

~

I found Savannah very quickly once I got to the beach. The sun was setting, and there were already quite a few people there. The bonfire was lit, and its flames were dancing. There was music playing from speakers at a nearby bar.

I dragged Savannah over to grab a drink. The drinking age on the island was twenty-one, so I ordered a mocktail. Savannah did the same.

While we waited for our drinks, we scoped the beach for cute guys. Savannah seemed to have a good eye for them, and pointed out a dozen in just a few minutes. I knew Savannah was hoping to be asked to dance, but I also knew she wasn't opposed to asking one of the guys herself.

As for me, I actually *could* dance. It could even be considered one of my "good qualities". I was a little bit happy that Ryan planned on coming later. I wanted to show him I could, in fact, do something right.

When our mocktails arrived, we each took a sip. Mine tasted really good. Pineapple and mango flavours danced on my tongue, making me hungry for more.

When we finished our drinks, we went off to dance. Our game plan was to start off dancing together, and wait and see if someone came along to pull us away from each other.

When I was younger, I had complained when my Mom insisted I take those tango classes, but I wasn't complaining now. I was so glad to be able to put that knowledge to good use.

Savannah instantly noticed that I knew how to move on the dance floor. Compared to the weird fist pumping thing she was doing, I was moving like a ballroom dance pro.

"Wow, you have some *moves,* Aubany," Savannah noticed. "You look amazing!"

I couldn't help but grin at her as I twirled. The sky had started to get dark, which caused a soft glow to illuminate us from the lights at the bar and the bonfire.

Not long after, as I was starting to lose myself in the music, a tall guy with dark curly hair came over and asked Savannah if she would like to dance. I gave her an encouraging nod, and she went off with him.

Now I was alone on the dance floor, but I wasn't particularly sad about it. There were some moves I wasn't able to do with a partner nearby, ad now that I was solo, I could really get into it.

As I moved through the blur of people around me, I caught sight of the bar. Sitting there was Ryan, watching me.

I ignored him and continued dancing, but now I felt a tad self-conscious. I glanced back, and his eyes were still on me.

149

I couldn't help but smile smugly at him. Who had good qualities now? I raised my eyebrows as a challenge and threw myself back into the flurry of music and dancing. I danced for a few more minutes, purposely choosing moves I knew well to show off a little, and glanced back.

But he was gone.

A flutter of disappointment settled in me. I felt almost stupid for trying to show off in front of him. It was like someone had stuck a nail in my heart. Clearly he hadn't been watching me after all. Either that, or I hadn't been as dazzling as I originally thought.

Frowning, I turned back to the crowd, only to come face to face with him.

"I didn't know you could dance like that," he said softly, almost breathlessly.

A cascade of emotions went through me: pride, satisfaction, amusement, anticipation.

"I told you—you don't know me well enough to know everything about me," I replied with a smile.

"Can I dance with you?" he asked quickly.

"Oh, what's this? *The* Ryan Rupert wants to dance with the weak girl who's scared of the ocean and can't do a thi—"

He pressed his finger to my lips. "Don't say that. Not anymore," he said. "I should *never* have said that."

"Well, I thought you were just stating facts," I said teasingly. I was feeling brilliant. *I* had the upper hand this time. He was completely mesmerised by my appearance and the way I could move, and I was *so* using it to my full advantage.

"It doesn't matter," he said. "Everyone has their flaws, just like you said. And considering your bravery in diving earlier today, I don't think I can call you those things anymore," he said.

He took my hand and led me to start dancing with him. I felt a thrill, and I wasn't sure if it was from him holding my waist or the fact that I'd made him so vulnerable.

"Then what kind of things will you call me?" I asked.

"Courageous," he replied. "Witty."

"Go on," I breathed.

"Beautiful," he said, keeping his gaze locked on mine.

I smiled. Ha!

"I think I found one of your flaws," I said, keeping my voice soft and teasing.

"Really? What is it?" he asked, looking genuinely curious as a smile crept across his face.

"You are too easily swayed by looks," I said, before stepping away from him and shooting him a teasing smile. "I don't fall for guys that easily, Rupert."

He stared at me with shocked eyes as I escaped through the crowd of people, giddy with satisfaction.

Oh, that had been *fun*! No wonder he always teased me. I didn't realise finding a person's weak points could be so enjoyable!

I headed to the bar to order another mocktail, still smiling. Another girl came up to the bar and ordered a Bloody Mary. She had brown hair and wore a slim, green dress. She leaned on the bar next to me, as she waited for her drink.

I noticed her bracelet, which was gold and had small green hearts hanging from it.

"I like your bracelet," I said all of a sudden. I have this thing about randomly giving people compliments. I didn't *mean* to start a conversation with a random girl at the bar, it kind of just happened.

She turned to me. "Thanks," she said slowly. She gave me a once over. "I like your shoes," she offered.

"Thanks," I replied, laughing nervously.

I was about to introduce myself, but her drink arrived and she took it. Without another word, she headed off into the crowd again.

When my drink was ready, I sipped it and searched the crowd for Savannah from my spot at the bar. I figured she'd gone off somewhere with that guy. I hoped he didn't turn out to be a creep or anything.

Feeling a little worn out, I decided to head back to the room—once I finished my drink. As much as I loved my dress, I kind of wanted to get out of it. I always felt more comfortable in a pair of shorts.

I headed along the path past the pools, back towards our accommodation. As I was walking near the pools, I looked out onto the lit-up water. It was so calm. So unlike the ocean. Pool water was comforting and peaceful—safe even. Ocean water was unpredictable.

Suddenly, something shoved me from behind, and I toppled towards the water. But just as I was about to fall in, someone grabbed me.

I turned around and came face to face with Ryan, holding me in his arms.

"Just kidding. Like I'd let you fall in again," he said, smirking.

I frowned. "Was it really necessary to push me?" I asked.

"Well, it got your attention," he replied.

"Have you ever heard of the word 'Hello?' Or even just tapping someone on the shoulder to let them know you're there?"

"But where's the fun in that?" Ryan asked slyly. He steadied me and then let go.

I realised something then—Ryan was just like the ocean. Unpredictable. Terrifying, at times. But I also realised I was starting to like them both.

"Are you going back to the room?" I asked him.

"I was. Is that where you were going?" he replied, looking curious.

"Yeah," I said. "I need to get out of this dress."

"I agree," Ryan replied.

I raised an eyebrow. "I thought you liked this dress," I said slowly.

We began walking, side by side, at a steady pace.

"I do," Ryan replied. "But it's driving me insane. For a moment, I really considered letting you hit that water."

"Oh, here we go again with the cheesy stuff," I said, walking ahead of him.

"I wasn't trying to anger you earlier," he called, running to keep up. "I was being serious about why I pushed you the first time."

"Look, Ryan," I said, stopping to face him. "I don't think you get this, but you've really left a mark on my feelings with all the teasing you've put me through over the years. If you think you can change that so easily, you're wrong. But if you have any intention of changing it at all, you might want to start by cutting out all the horrible, snarky comments."

"Okay," he said.

I froze, shocked.

He gave me a serious look and added, "From this moment on I'll stop with the rude comments. I promise."

I narrowed my eyes. I didn't reply as we continued along the path towards the cabin. It was hard to believe him, but I supposed I didn't have to. If he really wanted to change things, he would have to earn my trust back. Whether he succeded would depend on his ability to keep his word.

CHAPTER TEN

LOVE-HATE RELATIONSHIP

When morning came, I groggily opened my eyes. It took me a few moments to wake up properly, and I used this time to check my phone. I had three texts from Savannah. In all of them she gushed about the cute boy she'd met last night and insisted I call her so she could tell me all about it.

I looked over to Ryan's bed and, to my surprise, he was still asleep. Usually he was up well before me. I hadn't had the opportunity to see him asleep before. He looked kind of peaceful, and I didn't want to disturb him, so I crept over to the balcony and quietly slipped outside.

When Savannah answered the phone, she sounded excited.

"Oh, you're never going to believe it! I had the best night last night!" she said, giggling. "Aubany, he was so *dreamy*, and we went back to his room, and—
"

"Whoa, please spare me the details of what you and *dreamy boy* got up to in his room," I said quickly. "Was he nice, at least? He didn't hurt you, right?"

"Aubany, he's *amazing*. His name is Alex, and I'm seeing him again later. But I just can't get my mind off him and I need something to distract me until then. Do you want to hang out?"

I wanted to point out that I was supposed to be a friend, not a distraction, but I let it slide. I thought about the activities left on the island that we hadn't tried, still hoping to avoid water activities if possible.

"How about we play mini-golf?" I suggested finally.

"That sounds perfect. I'll meet you at the docks?" she asked.

"Sure. I'll be there in twenty minutes," I said. I headed inside, still trying to keep as quiet as possible.

I took a very quick shower and was about to leave, when I thought of something.

I hesitated, not sure if I should do it, but then I decided *Oh hell, why not?,* and pulled out a mug and the coffee jar.

A few moments later, there was a steaming cup of coffee on Ryan's bedside table, and I was out the door.

~

Pualani Island was the only island connected to the main island by a bridge, and I was thankful for that. We took a golf cart over because the walk would have taken forever.

Ordinary golf bored me to no extent, but mini golf was pretty interesting. I mean, maybe it was my inner child coming out, but there was something fun about whacking a ball through tunnels and over cute little bridges.

Still, miniature-sized or not, it didn't change the fact that I had terrible aim, and I hit the ball into the nearby pond at least three times. By the time I was going back for my fourth ball, the guy at the desk stopped giving me the pink ones in fear that I'd lose them all.

Then, when we were about halfway through the course, Savannah managed to get her ball wedged in a pipe, which we *thought* was part of the course, but apparently wasn't. We spent ten minutes trying to find a stick long and sturdy enough to poke it out with. Just when things were starting to look grim for Savannah's ball, we heard a voice behind us.

"Why don't you just use the end of your golf club?"

I spun around and, to my surprise, came face to face with the girl from last night. Her eyes studied us as we realised that what she said was actually a pretty smart idea.

"Why didn't we think of that?" I asked Savannah.

"I know," she replied, looking embarrassed. We turned to the girl.

"Thanks," I said. She knelt down, angled her own golf club as if she was playing pool, and poked the

160

ball out. It went flying over the course and landed in the grass nearby. With a smile, she straightened up and introduced herself.

"I'm Courtney."

We told her our names, and Savannah invited her to play the rest of the course with us. She accepted. We didn't run into any other problems as we finished the remaining holes. I noticed that Courtney had pretty good aim. She also seemed nice enough, but there was something about her I couldn't put my finger on. Then again, it might have just been intimidation from how pretty she was.

~

There was a café outside the miniature golf course. By the time we'd finished playing, we were starving, so all three of us decided to grab a bite to eat.

The café had super yummy-looking smoothies and I eagerly ordered one. We all decided to share a large plate of fried. I sipped on my smoothie as we waited for them to arrive, and Savannah started chatting with Courtney. I could tell the two of them were going to be fast friends.

You know when you meet someone, and you just know you're not going to get along with them, even though you can't pinpoint the reason why because there doesn't seem to be anything wrong with them? Well, that was the case with me and Courtney. So while she and Savannah were comparing the best places to buy shoes, I sat staring out at the ocean through the glass windows like I was far too intellectual for their conversation.

After our fries arrived and we started eating, Savannah had an idea.

"Hey, we should go island hopping after lunch!" she suggested.

"Yeah! That sounds like fun," Courtney said.

"Count me out," I held up my hands in protest. "I'm beginning to think that boats are at the root of my problem, so there's no way I want to spend the afternoon hopping on and off them."

"Oh, Aubany," Savannah said sadly. "Come on, it will be fun. Island hopping isn't nearly as bad as diving. We'll be on the islands more than we'll be on the water," she promised.

Courtney was watching me with a confused expression.

"I'm afraid of the sea," I explained, to clear things up for her.

"Why?" she asked.

I thought about that for a minute. I could list a number of good reasons, but it's not like I chose to be scared of the ocean. It's just one of those things. Everyone's afraid of something, right? So I found it hard to explain where my fear of the ocean had stemmed from, even if I suspected "Titanic" *might* have had something to do with it . . .

So I simply answered with, "I just don't know what's in it. Or trust it, for that matter."

Savannah was now giving me a pleading expression, like she really wanted me to come along. "Just for a little while," she insisted. "Maybe this will be good for you. It might stop Ryan from teasing you so much."

"Oh, that's another thing," I said quickly. "He's being *nice* to me. Can you believe it?"

"What's this?" Savannah smirked. "He's a *nice guy* now, huh?"

"Who's Ryan?" Courtney asked.

"He's only Aubany's super hot, yet super annoying neighbour, who she's trapped with on this . . . how did she put it? *Nightmare island from hell!*" Savannah said.

"It's not *that* bad," I said quickly. "I was just being a little dramatic those first few days."

"Super hot?" Courtney asked, like that had been the only thing she'd heard.

"Yes, but, he's not as dreamy as Alex," Savannah stated, pointing a fry at us. She popped it in her mouth and a strange, goofy smile crossed her face.

"Oh dear," I muttered, watching her. "I guess we're not being distracting enough, huh? Okay, no more boy talk. It's time to take you island hopping."

"So, does this mean you'll come?" Savannah asked excitedly.

I rolled my eyes.

"I don't think I have a choice," I sighed. We paid for our meal and headed back to the main island to rent our own dingy.

~

As we set out, I realised that boat rides were starting to grow on me, very slowly. When I was on them, I still felt sick and nauseous, but once I got off, that feeling would instantly disappear, which meant no vomiting.

The Lanikai Islands were the perfect place for island hopping. There wasn't much there, except for Josh and Renee's accommodation and their accompanying pools. It was mainly a spot of tropical beauty that had been left untouched.

Large, leafy ferns and towering palm trees greeted us as we meandered along the white, sandy beaches. I kept an eye out for crabs and other dangerous creatures, but luckily, we didn't run into any. We did find a rock pool, and I peered at it from a distance while Courtney and Savannah went digging in it for shells.

As we reached the end of one beach, we came across a cave. It looked dark, and eerie, and my only thoughts were to stay the heck out of it, but Courtney seemed to have a daring sense of adventure and was all up for exploring.

"Let's go check out what's in there!" she said. I was praying that Savannah would protest, but she was up for it too.

"I'll just wait out here," I told them, hugging my arms. "You've probably gathered I'm not really the adventurous type."

"Oh, really?" came a teasing voice from behind me. "What happened to your *thrill-seeking* side, Aubs?"

I turned around and spotted Ryan, leaning against a palm tree with a smirk on his face.

"Where the heck did *you* come from?" I asked.

"I was visiting Mom and Dad, and then I noticed you guys over here so I thought I'd see what you were up to. And I'm glad I did, because I'm *so* up for exploring a cave."

He walked over to us and shot me a smug smile. He held out his hand, like he expected me to grab it.

"Come on, Aubs, I won't let the scary monsters get you," he promised, his eyes teasing.

I narrowed my eyes at him.

"I thought you were going to stop with the rude comments."

"Oh, come on, it's just a bit of light teasing," he replied.

"And since when do you call me "Aubs"?" I added, frowning.

He leaned closer. "Since you made me a coffee this morning. I feel like our relationship has really grown lately, don't you?"

I flushed red. I'd forgotten about that. Now I was kind of kicking myself for it. "I was just returning the favour," I muttered. He lightly patted my shoulder.

"Whatever you say," he grinned. He turned to Savannah and Courtney. Savannah was smiling at us in a way that was kind of unnerving me, and Courtney had that awestruck look on her face that most girls got when their eyes landed on Ryan.

"Now, why don't you lovely ladies lead the way while I pick up the rear to ensure Aubany doesn't escape on us?"

Savannah and Courtney were only too eager to head into the cave.

I grimaced. "Can't we at least get flashlights?" I asked, as we followed.

"Why? Want to check me out while we're in there?" he asked with a wink.

"No, but I'd like to see where I'm going at least," I snapped.

He pulled out his phone and switched it on, using it as a light.

"That's where these come in handy," he said.

I realised what a brilliant idea that was, and instantly copied him.

"What would you do without me?" he asked playfully.

"Well, I imagine I'd be doing something less terrifying," I replied bitterly.

"Oh, your enthusiasm simply dazzles me, Aubany," he said.

I ignored him.

We headed deeper into the cave, and, although our phones shed enough light to watch our step, they were pretty useless for seeing anything farther than a few inches ahead of us.

Which is why, when we came to a point where the cave split into two sections, I almost ran straight into a wall.

I stopped as soon as I realised the dark shadowy thing in front of me was solid, and pressed a hand against it. It was cold and moist.

"Ugh," I said, wiping my hand on my shorts. I took a few steps back and checked out the split section. Both ways appeared to be equal in terms of what could be mysteriously lurking in them.

"We should split up," Ryan said finally. "Aubany and I will go this way, and you two go that way. If you find anything cool, text. Or just yell out. You know, whatever works."

Or we could turn back, I thought.

Ryan steered me in one direction, and Savannah went off with Courtney, linked arm in arm. They reminded me of two happy, little schoolgirls. A streak of jealousy went through me.

"That's a scary expression on your face, Aubs," Ryan pointed out, shining his phone light at me.

I squinted. "Geez, will you point that thing elsewhere? I'm going blind here!" I protested, holding up a hand to shield my eyes.

He shined the light back towards the floor, and I shined mine ahead to ensure we didn't run into any more walls. We shared the light as we walked. I wasn't going to deny that I was beyond freaked out, and I needed something to put my mind at ease. I shuffled a little closer to Ryan, which made me feel slightly better.

Considering it was him, that was a *statement*.

"Who's the new girl?" Ryan asked finally.

"That's Courtney," I replied. "She's pretty nice. I met her last night at the bar."

Ryan nudged me. "You went off to make friends without me?" he pouted.

"I wouldn't consider her my friend. Although she and Savannah seem to be pretty chummy already. Guess it's just one of those things," I said.

"Well, don't feel too down. You've still got me," Ryan said with enthusiasm.

I snorted. "Yeah, because I so *love* hanging out with you, with all your snarky comments and endless teasing," I said.

"Oh come on, I'm not that bad," he protested.

"Have you seen yourself?" I asked pointedly.

"Of course. I check myself out in the mirror every morning," he replied, with a smirk that was only faintly visible in the light.

I scoffed. "You are unbelievable."

He suddenly stopped in his tracks.

I stared at him, confused. "What?" I asked.

"Shhh," he said quickly. He shone his phone light up the walls of the cave, looking around. "Do you hear that?"

"Hear what?" I asked, feeling nervous. I got the feeling he was just trying to scare me, but I stopped and listened. I could hear water dripping. And then I realised there was also a soft squeaking sound coming from somewhere. I slowly looked up. Ryan glanced up, too.

There were hundreds of them. Tiny, black things hanging from the ceiling. Our phone lights disturbed them, and in an instant a sea of glowing eyes appeared.

I was frozen in terror.

"Bats!" I finally shrieked. My scream startled them, causing them to take flight. They flapped around our heads, screeching. I ducked instinctively, covering my head with my arms.

"Come on!" Ryan said, grabbing my arm. He led us towards the cave exit. We sprinted, eager to escape.

When we finally made it outside again, the sunlight was blinding and it took our eyes a few moments to adjust. I collapsed onto a nearby log, panting.

"I can't believe you made me go in there!" I said to Ryan. He took a seat next to me, smoothing his hair back carefully.

"Oh come on, wasn't it *thrilling*?" he teased.

I narrowed my eyes at him.

"Oh, I'm sure you loved it too, especially when those bats ruined your hairdo," I said, reaching over to ruffle his hair, effectively ruining it again.

He groaned.

"Aubany!" he protested.

I smirked. As he continued to try and fix it, I noticed Savannah and Courtney emerging from the cave.

"We heard a scream," Savannah said, coming over to us. "We got worried so we came back."

I explained about the bats.

"Gross!" Savannah said. "There wasn't anything like that on our side. Just a lot of moss."

Savannah's phone suddenly went off, and she checked it. "Oh, it's Alex!" she gushed. "Our cruise is in an hour. I have to go get ready," she said. She came over and hugged me. "Thanks for hanging out with me today."

"It's no problem," I replied. Savannah and Court-ney also hugged, which made me jealous again. They'd become friends so fast.

As Savannah headed off, Courtney turned to us.

"Well, I'd love to stay and hang out with you guys more," she said. "But I also have to be some-where. We should do this again sometime."

"Sure," I replied, just to be polite. In reality, I had no intention of exploring any more caves as long as I lived. She headed off towards the resort, where the docks were.

P.S.Malcolm

Which left Ryan and me alone.

Ryan was looking up at the sky and frowning. "It looks like there's a storm brewing over there," he said.

I looked up and realised he was right. The sky was filled with black clouds that were heading our way. I gulped.

"We'd better get back before it gets any closer," I said. With that, we headed off.

CHAPTER ELEVEN

THUNDER AND LIGHTNING, VERY FRIGHTENING

By the time we got back to the room, I could see lightning flashes outside. I tried not to show how much they were getting to me. The last thing I needed was Ryan finding out I had another fear.

"Should we order in tonight?" Ryan suggested. He was reading the menu on the fridge. "We could order pizza and share it."

"You want to share a pizza with me?" I asked.

"Well, why not?" he asked.

I smiled a little.

"Okay," I agreed.

Ryan called reception to place the order, and I tried to keep myself from peering nervously out the window. Once Ryan got off the phone, he glanced over at me.

"What's with the anxious look?" he asked.

"What are you talking about?" I squeaked.

He frowned. "You don't think I'm going to do something to the pizza, do you?" he asked. I rolled my eyes.

"Of course not," I replied.

"Well, stop pacing then. You're freaking me out," he said. I hadn't even realised I'd been pacing at all. I quickly went to the bed and sat down, trying not to fidget.

"You've been fairly nice today," I said finally.

"You're the one who asked me to be," he replied. "You seemed less moody today, yourself."

"It's kind of weird how we're having a normal conversation, and not bickering," I said. "But it's also kind of nice."

"What, you don't like our fights?" Ryan asked, with a teasing look.

I frowned. "Not when they get out of hand. I mean, I can live with you making fun of me I guess, but not when you start going on and on about how much I suck at stuff."

He paused. "I guess I can see how that would get annoying." He smiled.

Then I remembered something. "Back in Florida before we left, you said that you'd rather drown yourself than ever get along with me," I said. "Yet, here you are, being nice to me."

"That was a dramatic statement. And a stupid one," Ryan replied. "I find your company quite nice, which was surprising to learn."

"So you didn't mean it when you said it?" I asked quietly.

He hesitated.

"You don't have to lie to me, Ryan. I was experiencing quite similar thoughts at the time."

"I was overreacting . . . but I guess the meaning behind the words was true," he said quietly. "I was annoyed that my summer vacation was getting hijacked. But that's different now. I didn't know you." His expression was filled with honesty.

"You still don't know me," I pointed out.

"I'd *like* to get to know you," he said.

"Ryan . . ." I trailed off. "I . . . I think I'd like to get to know you, too. But no more pranks. I swear to God, my trust in you is thin and wavering as it is, and if you destroy what you've built over these past few days, it's not coming back."

He crossed over to me and knelt beside me.

"No more pranks," he promised, squeezing my hand. "There's something I'd like to continue to help you with, though."

"And what would that be?" I asked.

"Your fear of the ocean. You've made progress since getting on this island. I want to help you get over it completely before we leave."

"Why? What's the point?" I asked.

"Fears aren't good to hold onto. You should try and overcome them if you can. From what I've seen, I have absolute faith that you can get over yours," he said.

"How do you plan on helping me?" I asked slowly.

"We'll do more activities. I'll help you through them all," he said. "Think of it as a way for me to get to know you."

He had a point. I wasn't in a hurry to go diving again, but if I had to, I wouldn't be completely freaked out by the idea. That never would have happened without his help. And while going island hopping today had proven that nature was unpredictable, the sea didn't appear nearly as deadly as I had made it out to be. If he really wanted to help me, I guessed I should give it a go. I mean, what else was I going to do on this island for the next five weeks?

So I agreed. He looked pleased to hear it.

When our pizza arrived, we opened it up on the bed and sat together, eating. We turned on the TV and just talked about stuff that I never thought I'd ever talk about with Ryan Rupert.

The fact that we were having a conversation at all was pretty outstanding.

~

When it got late, we decided to go to bed. I changed in the bathroom and climbed under the sheets. Ryan had successfully distracted me from the fact that a storm had been brewing outside, but with the sudden silence in the room, I was now fully aware of its presence. I saw the lightning flashes. I heard the rain on the roof. And worst of all, I heard the thunder outside, shaking the cabin.

It only got louder and louder, making it impossible for me to sleep. After lying there with a pillow over my head for half an hour, a loud crack from the sky made me jump, and I knocked over a table lamp, which clattered to the floor. Ryan's light switched on.

"What happened?" he asked. He noticed my frightened expression. "Wait . . ." he trailed off. "Don't tell me . . . you're afraid of thunderstorms too, aren't you?"

I bent down to pick up the light. "Of course not! I was just reaching for something and accidentally knocked over the lamp."

Another crack made me jump.

He raised an eyebrow at me.

"Uh huh," he said slowly.

I groaned in annoyance. God, this was too embarrassing. I jumped out of bed and raced to the bathroom, locking myself in.

Now he had another thing to add to his list of my bad qualities. If this nice side of Ryan ever disappeared, he'd have even more ammunition to use against me. I couldn't believe how much this sucked.

Another flash of lightning lit up the bathroom. I huddled on the floor between the sink and the shower, and pretended it was all just a bad dream. I shut my eyes and put my hands over my ears

Usually, when there was a thunderstorm, I would plug in my iPod and let music drown out the sound. But I didn't have it with me.

I heard a knock at the door. "Aubany?"

I ignored him.

"Are you okay in there?" Ryan's voice echoed. I continued to ignore him.

He rattled the doorknob. "Can you please answer me? Or unlock the door at least?"

"I'm not coming out," I called.

"You can't stay in there all night," he pointed out. "At least, not alone."

I looked up. What did he mean by *that*?

"Will you *please* just open the door?" he begged. "Aubs?" His voice was soft.

I stood up slowly. There was a brief pause in the thunder and lightning so I quickly moved over to the door and unlocked it. He slipped inside and shut the door again.

"Aubs," he said again, softly, when he saw me. He looked concerned.

A loud crash of thunder made me scream. I shut my eyes and covered my ears, squatting down. I hated the fact that I looked so stupid in front of Ryan.

I felt something nudge my shoulder. I looked to my left and, to my surprise, Ryan had taken a seat next to me.

"So here we are, huddled in a bathroom," he said, with a small smile. "Did you really just lock yourself in here to avoid me?"

"Go ahead. Say something snarky, why don't you?" I challenged. "After all, it's only my life you're ruining."

"Wow. Harsh, Aubs," he said, taking my hand. "I wasn't going to tease you about it. I already said before that we're moving past that now."

It took me a few seconds to realize he was being serious. "I guess I'm still having a hard time trusting you," I admitted.

"Well, now that you know I'm not going to do that, do you plan on sitting in here all night? It's kind of cold, and miserable, sitting on a bathroom floor when there are beds out there," he said.

I was going to agree when a flash of lightning lit up the bathroom, followed by a rumble of deafening thunder. That was enough to glue me to the spot.

"I'm not going anywhere," I said quickly, covering my ears again. "At least not until I have a distraction of some kind."

"A distraction, huh?" came Ryan's muffled response, low and flirtatious. I flushed red as he waggled his eyebrows.

"Don't even go there," I warned, slowly uncovering my ears. He raised his hands in protest.

"Okay. Not gonna say it. Well, what do you usually do when storms hit?"

"Listen to music," I replied. "But my iPod's at home."

"I forgot mine too," Ryan admitted. "But I can sing to you, if you want?"

I stared at him.

Ryan Rupert? Singing? What was he going to bust out "Cosby Sweater" or something?

He saw my expression. "Relax. I'm actually pretty okay at it. Well, at least no one's told me otherwise," he said. His hand was still in mine, and his fingers were moving in slow circles over my palm.

He leaned closer and started singing softly in my ear.

To my surprise, he *didn't* start busting out Hilltop Hoods or Eminem, like I'd originally expected.

He started singing a song by the Jonas Brothers.

I burst out laughing, which caused him to break off singing and raise an eyebrow at me.

"What?" he asked gently. But I was too busy laughing to answer. A loud crack of thunder sounded and I didn't even jump.

"Did it sound bad?" he asked, frowning.

"No, it's just your choice of song," I replied, still giggling.

"It was the first thing that popped in my head!" he protested with a smile.

"Well, I think I just found one of your good qualities," I said. "Or maybe two. You have a good singing voice . . . and you're good at distracting me. And I suppose you have an okay taste in music," I said.

"That's more like three qualities," he pointed out.

Low thunder made me tense up again, and he started singing again. It was almost romantic, me huddled on the floor with him singing in my ear. A bit like being serenaded.

I could feel his warm breath tickling my ear, his voice low and alluring as he sang. He smelled of freshly scented soap and something that was distinctly Ryan. Every time thunder crashed overhead I felt myself pressing into his side a little more, and he would squeeze my hand a bit to reassure me.

Before long, his voice turned to a whisper, and I could feel his lips almost grazing my neck. And then they *were* on my neck, planting light, whispery kisses. I sighed softly, and turned my head turning towards his.

And then, suddenly, we were kissing. Quite hard. My hands tugged his shirt, pulling him closer to me, and he turned so he had me pressed against the bathroom door. I felt one of his hands cup my cheek, while the other traced the nape of my neck.

"Aubs," he whispered against my mouth.

His touch was like fire, shutting out everything else, making me completely forget about the storm.

That is, until thunder sounded overhead and I jumped, accidentally kneeing him in the shin.

I cursed, and he pulled away with a groan of annoyance.

"I'm sorry," I whispered quickly.

He shook his head. "Don't worry about it," he said quietly. His eyes met mine, and he broke into a smile. A legitimate, happy smile. "Did you just kiss me?" he asked, his expression smug. His eyes were lit up, excited.

I flushed red.

"I . . .um . . ." I stuttered. "I think . . . I should go back to bed now."

His smile wavered, but he let me stand up.

"Will you be okay with the thunder?" he asked.

"What? Oh yeah, I'll be fine," I said quickly, hurrying out of the bathroom. My emotions were swirling around in my chest like some crazy whirlpool. What on earth had I just done?

P.S.Malcolm

"Are you sure?" he asked, sounding genuinely concerned.

I nodded, shooting him a quick smile. "Positive. Thanks for . . . um . . . helping me. Goodnight, Ryan," I said, jumping into bed and turning away from him. I lay there very still, until the light blinked off and the room fell into darkness.

It wasn't that I hadn't wanted to kiss him, because clearly my actions had said otherwise. It was the fact that it was *him*, of all people, I'd fallen for.

A part of me still didn't trust him enough to know whether it was a huge trap or something legitimate. A girl could only take so much.

Being teased and taunted was one thing. But having your heart ripped out?

That was a whole new world of pain.

CHAPTER TWELVE

A CHAOTIC CRUISE

I hardly slept that night.

There were storms rumbling both internally and externally. The chemistry between me and Ryan had struck like lightning, and my emotions were now a chaotic mess. They battered into me like a rainstorm, constantly reminding me of their conflicting presence.

I had kissed Ryan Rupert. My lifelong enemy! And I had no idea how to feel about it. Should I be happy? Should I be terrified? What was going to happen now?

And just when I thought the ocean was the scariest thing I'd have to face all summer. . .

Luckily, I finally drifted off, and when I awoke the next morning, it was to clear, sunny skies. The humid scent of rainfall was in the air, mixed with coffee and the fresh soap that reminded me of Ryan.

I blinked. The curtains had been parted slightly, and the door was open a tad—just enough to let in the sun, but not enough to be a pain this early in the morning. Ryan was on the balcony, his back to me. On the table beside me sat a cup of coffee.

Normally, I would have smiled at the fact that he'd gone out of his way to make me coffee yet again, but this time I had no idea what to think. The memory of last night lingered in my brain, changing everything. That moment seemed to highlight all the subtext that had existed between us, and I knew it would ultimately reveal his true intentions, whether they were pure or pure evil.

I wanted to run outside and escape from him— clear my mind, protect myself while I still could. But I also wanted to stay, so I could wait and see what was going to happen next, and be in his company. I was confused, and I hated it.

Quietly as I could, I snuck over to the dresser and grabbed the first items of clothing I found, then slipped into the bathroom and locked myself in. At least I had the chance to be alone for a while in there, so I could collect my thoughts a little before I had to face him.

But since it was the place where it had happened, the memory was even stronger and more overpowering.

I pushed it to the back of my mind and got in the shower. I tried to ignore the soapy scent that Ryan had left behind. I decided to block it out by washing my hair. Soon the scent of apples had replaced it, and I relaxed a little.

When I'd finished showering, I took a deep breath and walked out.

Ryan had come back inside. His gaze met mine and I quickly looked away, which, I'm sure, only confused *him*.

I occupied myself by making my bed, and my eyes rested on the coffee he'd left me. I didn't want to waste it, so I took it and gingerly sipped it. I snuck a glance at Ryan again.

"Morning," he said quietly. He looked as awkward as I felt.

"Hi," I replied.

He was leaning on the counter, looking like he wanted to say something but not sure how to say it. Eventually he just ran a hand through his hair and reached for his wallet.

"I'll see you down at breakfast," he said finally. I nodded, and he headed for the door.

When I heard it click shut, I exhaled a long sigh. I was so scared of what was happening between us. It was like we'd finally started getting along, and now our relationship was even more fragile than it was before. If we started fighting again, we were going to hate each other even more. And, if things didn't go well, it was going to be so awkward, having to share the room for the rest of the trip.

But then again, if it wasn't real and he was just playing with my emotions, I knew I was going to get hurt. I'd really started to like this new Ryan, and if he turned out to be a fake, I was sure I'd crumble into pieces.

Why did we have to kiss?

I blamed the thunderstorm. My stupid fears were ruining my life. *Just* when I was beginning to tackle my fear of the ocean, one of my other fears had to go and wreak havoc!

With a sigh, I finished the coffee and headed out to breakfast.

~

When I got there, I spotted Savannah and Courtney sitting together at a table. The last thing I wanted to do was watch them bond even further, but it was either that, sit awkwardly with Ryan, or sit alone like a total loser.

I grabbed some cereal and headed over to them.

"Hey, Aubany!" Savannah said brightly. I took a seat and smiled at both of them.

"How was your cruise?" I asked Savannah.

"It was cancelled!" Savannah complained, "Because of the storm. But that's okay, because it's been rescheduled for tonight. Still, I hear a lot of people dropped their spots. I guess that's the bad thing about planning activities ahead of time," she said.

"I made a booking, seeing as there was space," Courtney added.

"Well, I hope it actually goes ahead this time," I said.

Savannah suddenly looked distracted and sat up straighter. "Alex!" she called, waving someone over. I turned my head and saw the curly haired dude from the dance thingy coming over to us. He had a charming smile.

"Good morning," he said, bending down to peck Savannah on the lips. I turned away, resisting the urge to gag. It was too early for kissing, and too soon, after last night, to be reminded of it. "Alex, this is Aubany," Savannah offered. I said hello. She pointed to Courtney and introduced her as well, as Courtney smiled politely.

I thought that Alex might go off after that, but he decided to pull up a chair and hold hands with Savannah as they shared breakfast. (Yuck!)

"So, what should we do today?" Savannah asked all of us. "I mean, the cruise isn't until tonight."

"We could just chill out at the pool. Have a relaxing day," Courtney suggested.

"Aubany? You want to join us?" Savannah asked.

Gee, which would I prefer? The company of a cutesy couple and a nerve-wracking friend stealer, or the company of my former enemy whom I kissed and made things awkward with?

While I could have just hung out on my own all day, I decided that being alone would be more toxic to my emotional state than the other two options, so I accepted Savannah's offer to chill with them.

After breakfast, we headed off to the Aqua Lagoon. I had to make a short detour back to the room to grab my swimsuit first, but I didn't run into Ryan, which was a relief.

It was beautiful there. The lagoon was beneath the Jungle Wing, which was perched on a cliff. A waterfall fell from the cliff straight into the lagoon itself. It was bordered on either side by a curtain of ivy that concealed a cave. The edges of the lagoon were outlined with rocks.

The day was sweltering hot after the storm, which made it the perfect day for swimming. Savannah and Alex were all over each other in the pool, jumping on each other's backs and splashing one another. Courtney sat by the edge and dangled her feet in, only slipping in from time to time to cool herself down. I just swam around, trying to distract myself from my thoughts.

Eventually, Alex went off to get ice cream for Savannah and the rest of us, and Courtney slipped off to the ladies room, leaving Savannah and I alone. She came gliding over to me in the water.

"You seem a little off today," she noted. "What's up?"

A part of me didn't want to talk about it. But another part did. I knew that it would be better for me to voice my feelings than bottle them all up like some secret, so I decided to confess.

"Ryan kissed me last night," I said.

This caused Savannah to squeal, and I suddenly found myself regretting my decision a little.

"Oh my God! I *knew* you two would! I knew it!" she said excitedly.

"But now it's awkward," I said. "We're supposed to hate each other, and I'm afraid he's only pretending. For all I know, this could be another one of his pranks," I said.

"Well, did it feel like he was pretending?" she asked.

I paused. " No," I admitted. "But he could be a good actor. I just . . . I don't trust him. Not yet. Not enough to be okay with this."

"Well, I think you should tell him that. Tell him exactly how you feel, before it gets any more awkward," Savannah said. "If he's serious, he'll wait until you're ready. And you can take all the time you need to figure out if he's lying or not."

"But what if I don't figure it out, and then it turns out that he is?" I asked.

"I think you'll be able to tell. These things have a way of working themselves out," Savannah promised. "Just go with your gut."

I hesitated, and the look on my face must've said all the rest.

"Hey," Savannah said gently. "Clearly you like him. That's a start. If you didn't, you wouldn't even be stressing over this. You'd be telling him to back off. And if you like him, well, chances are he probably likes you too. For real."

"You're right," I said. "I'll talk to him," I decided, nodding. I felt quite a bit better after talking to Savannah about it. She smiled, like she was happy she'd helped.

I knew I had to talk to Ryan sooner rather than later, so I headed back to the cabin in search of him. But when I got there, he was out.

Of course.

I could have called him, but I decided to just wait for him to come back. I was avoiding it again—putting it off. . . but I couldn't help it.

Talking about my feelings was a pretty scary thing, after all.

I lazed around on my bed, watching TV while I waited. I could have read, but I knew I wouldn't be able to concentrate in that frame of mind.

When the door finally swung open, I tensed and sat up straighter. Ryan came in and saw that I was there.

"Hey," he said.

"Hi," I said. The nervousness was back. The intensity in my chest was restricting and tight.

As if his presence wasn't bad enough, he looked me straight in the eyes, which just made the tightening in my chest ten times worse.

I pushed myself off the bed, eager to be doing something other than panicking. "Um . . ." I trailed off, trying to get the words out.

"Um?" he mused, with a small smile.

I was so relieved he was trying to humour me. Any other day I would have glared at him for it, but it brought a sense of normalcy back to us and I found myself letting out a small laugh.

"I need to talk to you," I managed finally.

"I figured. I kind of want to talk to you too," Ryan said. We kept our distance from one another across the room.

"So . . . um . . . we kissed," I blurted out.

I'd intended for the words to come out a little smoother, perhaps less straightforward. . . but it seemed to do the trick, because he nodded.

"Yeah," he said.

"And . . . I . . . um . . ." I paused. "Well . . . I just . . . I can't," I stammered.

I stopped myself and took a deep breath. I didn't want to say it bluntly, but how else could I tell him how I felt?

"I . . . sort of . . . don't trust you," I said finally. "I'm . . . well, I'm scared. Of what you might do to me. Because of our past. You've never been kind to me, and I'm terrified this is just another trick of yours."

"Aubs," he said, crossing the room. I held up my hands.

"No, just stay there," I said quickly. The last thing I needed was his proximity getting to me. He stopped in his tracks and nodded.

"I don't want to get hurt," I continued. "And I felt like I needed to tell you this . . . before something else happens or this turns awkward. I'm not saying I didn't like the kiss. I just . . . I can't kiss you again. At least, not until I'm sure you aren't messing with me."

It suddenly occurred to me that, now that he was *aware* I was afraid, it would give him all the more reasons to trick me, if that was his plan.

But when I saw his expression, and how gloomy he seemed, I forgot about that.

"I understand," he said. "I completely get it. It wasn't fair of me to tease you all these years. So I deserve to be suspected. I won't try and kiss you again," he promised.

"Thank you," I said, relieved.

"But I'm not going to give up on you," he said. "I'm going to do everything it takes to make you trust me. Because I want to show you that it's okay to trust me."

"You'll have to work pretty hard to persuade me," I said softly. I sat down.

"I will," he promised, looking determined. "Aubany, I could tell you why I spent all those years teasing you, but I have a feeling you wouldn't believe me right now. I didn't realise how much damage I did to you. But I promise that, when the time is right, I'll explain my actions. And until then, I'm going to work to gain your trust."

"Okay," I said. I couldn't imagine how I looked right now, but if it was anything like how I felt, I probably seemed vulnerable and weak—the very two things I wished I didn't show in front of Ryan, the very two things I wished I could prove to him I wasn't.

And if we weren't in such a weird place at that moment, I probably could have used a hug from him.

I certainly wasn't expecting what he did next.

"Do you want to go on a cruise?" he asked. I raised an eyebrow.

"A cruise?" I repeated. "You mean, purposely ride on a boat for longer than I need to?"

"I mean, confront your fear while doing something fun at the same time," he said. "Cruises are supposed to be relaxing. Enjoyable. They're not thrilling, like diving and exploring caves. I thought it might be another good way for you to fight your fear," he explained.

"Are you going to make me do it?" I asked.

204

"Well, I wouldn't say it like that. More like, I strongly *encourage* you to do it," he replied.

"When's this cruise?" I asked.

"Tonight," he replied. "They had extra room, so I already made the bookings."

Why did that not surprise me? *Typical* Ryan . . .

"That means we're on the same cruise as Savannah and the others," I said, which was probably a good thing. If Ryan pulled some kind of stunt, I'd have backup at least.

I sighed. "Alright. Fine. I guess we can try it," I said, which made him smile.

~

I was freaking out as we headed up the ramp. Even with Ryan beside me, I felt terrified. It wasn't just that boats made me queasy. Being on them for long periods of time made me paranoid that we were going to sink. Again, I clearly never should've watched *Titanic*.

The cruise would take two hours, as it toured around all the islands. It took place at night, so passengers could see the islands all lit up. According to Ryan, there was a day cruise as well.

When we got on the boat, I couldn't feel the rocking motion as much, maybe because this boat was bigger than the others I'd been on. The fact that it was dark meant I couldn't see the ocean, which was also a plus.

However, I could still hear it sloshing below against the boat.

I followed Ryan as he led me inside. There were lights everywhere, sparkling and dazzling. The tables were decorated with little red flowers and white tablecloths. Ryan and I took a seat.

There were huge windows on all sides that allowed us to see the ocean no matter where we sat.

I spotted Savannah and Alex across the room, giggling and holding hands. Ryan was reading a menu.

"After we've eaten, we can head upstairs to the deck for a better view," Ryan told me.

"That sounds good," I replied.

When the boat finally left the dock, it was slow and steady. My stomach had never felt so calm on a boat before. I opened up my own menu and began reading it. I decided to settle for a simple meal, in case my stomach decided to act up later.

Once Ryan and I ordered, we were left to face each other.

"How's your Mom?" he asked.

"She's okay. I've been meaning to call her again. I'll probably do that tomorrow," I told him.

"I like your Mom," he said. "She's a kind person."

I smiled. It was nice to hear him say that about her.

"How do you feel about . . . about her getting cancer?" he asked tentatively, like he wasn't sure if he should bring up the subject.

"Oh . . ." I trailed off, taken aback. "Um . . . well . . . it's been hard."

I paused, trying to think of the right words to say to him. He waited, not saying anything.

"She's never said that she's in pain or anything . . . she acts like she's fine. Like she's *going* to be fine and that she'll be home soon. And . . . while it's comforting to hear, I'm scared to face reality. But I know I have to eventually. I keep *trying* to understand everything but . . . it hurts to. It's so much easier to shut it all out but . . . I feel *awful* for shutting *her* out."

"You make it sound like she's not coming home," Ryan said, sounding concerned.

"No . . . uh, that's not what I meant," I said quickly. "No, I *know* there's every chance she *might* . . . but I know she might *not* as well. And if she *doesn't* . . . I don't even know how to think about that, let alone handle it if it happens. I don't *want* to think about that! But the more I think about the fact that she has *cancer* . . . the more I *have* to think about that."

There was a silence. I was almost expecting Ryan to apologise for even mentioning it, but his next words surprised me.

"Do you remember the time my *abuela* and *abuelo* came over from Barcelona?"

I'd forgotten Ryan's grandparents were Spanish. Josh was actually Spanish, so Ryan was *half* Spanish, but being raised in America, he didn't follow a lot of Spanish customs and only knew basic Spanish in order to communicate with his grandparents over the phone. It was easy to forget that about Ryan, considering how *American* he'd grown up to be.

"Yeah," I replied, wondering why he'd changed the topic to that. "Your parents invited us over for a barbeque and your grandma—uh, I mean *abuela*— kept saying how your cousin had just had her *quinciañera* and she wouldn't stop showing me pictures."

"Right. Your Mom drank *so* much wine that night that she got drunk and sang karaoke on the dining table. We took a video, remember?"

I started laughing. "That's right, she *did*!" I exclaimed. I'd completely forgotten.

"And the time she tried to cook us that birthday cake and used icing sugar instead of flour?"

I realised what Ryan was doing. He was trying to distract me from all the bad thoughts of my Mom, and remind me of all the memories I had of her. A feeling of warmth spread throughout my chest. We spent ages talking about her, and that led to other memories.

Somehow, Ryan seemed to be able to come up with plenty of good ones, while all I had were bad ones. Maybe I just had a habit of fixating on the negatives in everything.

I noticed that the awkwardness between us had settled, like dust. It had been everywhere—in the air—earlier today, but now it was calm. It was still there, but it was no longer stirring up and causing a mess.

When the boat had moved a bit off shore, I glanced out the window and gasped. It was *beautiful*.

All the islands twinkled like tiny golden stars, so it looked like we were surrounded by a sea of lights on every side.

"Wow," I breathed.

"I thought you might like it," Ryan said, smiling. "I was kind of hoping we could do the whole red wine thing too, but I left my fake ID at home."

I wasn't sure if he was joking, but I laughed anyway.

"Well, it's the thought that counts, right?" I said, which made him grin.

"I like what you're wearing," he said suddenly. I had no dresses other than the white one, so I'd chosen to wear a turquoise tank top with white flowers and silver sequins embellished along the top, and a white skirt with a silver belt.

Dinner went smoothly, and I managed to keep it all down this time.

When we finished eating, Ryan offered me his hand and we made our way upstairs to the deck. The air was slightly cooler up there, and the view a little brighter. I could make out soft hills in the darkness, and trees along the beaches.

It suddenly occurred to me that the whole cruise had been pretty romantic. The dining tables were a step up from the other restaurant, what with all the flowers and pretty tablecloths and lighting, and the stunning view was simply enchanting.

I felt my insecurities creeping back in. If any guy was trying to make me fall for him, wouldn't this be the way to do it? I mean, the whole experience was kind of overwhelming and could easily make you forget everything else.

I suddenly found myself very glad there hadn't been any wine involved, or I knew my resolve would never have lasted. We were leaning on the handrail, and Ryan's fingers were still laced with mine.

Well played, Rupert, I found myself thinking, but I couldn't let myself be so easily swayed. I unlaced my fingers and clasped them together in front of me, for good measure.

"Do you like the cruise?" he asked.

"Yes. It's lovely," I replied.

"How's your fear going? Are you feeling sick?"

"No," I said. I looked closely at him. He looked genuinely curious. Everything about him seemed so *genuine* now. Maybe I was worrying about nothing. Maybe all the insecurities were in my head, and there was nothing to fear at all.

Suddenly, there was a high-pitched sound, like something was tearing through metal. An abrupt lurching motion sent me stumbling sideways. I clutched the railing, sheer panic sweeping through me.

My eyes were wide with fear as I glanced at Ryan. "That's not supposed to happen, right?" I asked, my voice high and shrill. He looked worried too, which didn't reassure me in the slightest.

"No. It's not," he agreed. We raced back downstairs and found everyone standing and looking around worriedly. Loud chatter filled the air. The calm atmosphere from before had completely vanished. Another loud sound exploded from below, and the boat began to tilt.

"Ladies and gentlemen," a voice echoed through the speakers. "Please remain calm, and follow staff instructions immediately."

"What is happening?" I asked Ryan, clutching his arm in panic.

"I don't want to scare you," he said, his face pale, "But I think we're going down."

CHAPTER THIRTEEN

YOU WISH, JELLYFISH

The staff ordered us to grab lifejackets from cupboards along the sides of the room. They were helping us fasten them and telling us not to push. It was very hard to fight the urge not to. I just wanted to get off this thing, fast.

Ryan was holding my hand tightly.

Once we got our lifejackets on, they told us to head to the side of the boat, where the lifeboats were. There were tons of people scrambling for the exits, and I felt myself getting pushed and shoved in the crowd.

"This was *not* meant to happen," Ryan said, sounding annoyed. We found Savannah, Courtney and Alex outside, and we went over to them.

"What do you think's happened?" I asked.

"Well, we can't have hit an iceberg," Savannah replied reassuringly. "And we won't freeze, Aubany. The water will be warm, and we can swim to shore if we have to. We just need to get off this boat."

The lifeboats were filling up quickly. If we were lucky, no one would have to swim to shore. As we got closer to the front of the line, I overheard one of the staff members talking to another.

"The captain was just in the engine room," he said in a low voice. "There's a gaping hole in the side of the boat, and it looks like it was made by *someone*, rather than *something*."

"Who would purposely take down a cruise ship?" the other wondered.

That was a good question.

As I looked out at the water, I saw dozens of lifeboats heading to shore. The staff were bringing out the last of them now, and since there were only a few of us left, it looked like we weren't going to run out.

But as soon as they lowered the last few into the sea, they immediately began filling with water.

216

"There are holes in the last of them!" a female attendant exclaimed. She glanced nervously at the other staff members. "We'll have to swim," she said finally.

I gulped.

Ryan squeezed my hand reassuringly.

I had a lifejacket. I was going to be fine.

We both were.

The staff apologised to us and pointed us towards the stairs that led directly down the side of the boat to the water. It wasn't too far to shore. A few laps of a swimming pool, maybe. I had to take off my sandals, though.

The boat suddenly tipped even farther, and we all lost our balance and began to slide along the deck. Screaming, I tumbled along until I crashed into a metal staircase. I reached out and gripped the hand railing to stop myself from slipping further. Ryan had clutched onto a pole a little bit ahead of me.

"Get in the water, now!" the crew member bellowed, urging us to jump over the side of the boat before the boat sank completely. Guests began scrambling to the edge and flinging themselves over. They landed in the water and began to swim.

"Aubany!" Ryan called, urging me to follow.

I whimpered. "What if there are creatures?" "Worry about that later. If we don't go now, we don't go at all. We could get pulled under with the ship!" he replied urgently.

He offered me his hand and I reached out to grasp it. I felt his firm fingers curl around mine. He pulled me up towards him and grabbed my waist to keep me at his side.

"Together, okay?" he said. "I won't let anything hurt you. I promise."

I nodded. I noticed Savannah and Alex plunging off the side as we reached over to grab the edge. The boat tilted dangerously. Ryan threw his legs over, and I copied him, and then we jumped.

When we hit the water's surface, it felt cool—not freezing, just cool. I resurfaced and gasped for breath. Ryan appeared a few seconds later, his hair wet.

He turned to me. "Swim. Come on," he said.

We started pushing through the water, as fast as we could. We'd made it off just in time, as behind us, the boat made a loud shuddering noise and began to sink. I felt like crying and breaking down. My biggest fears had come to life.

Ryan suddenly stopped swimming.

"Shit," he said. I looked ahead and noticed it. There were dozens and dozens of jellyfish in the water in front of us—I'd barely been able to see them until Ryan had pointed them out. They were slowly creeping toward us. I glanced over and saw that Savannah and Alex and the rest of the swimmers had realised the same thing, and were swimming around them.

One came floating near us and I shrieked, clutching Ryan.

"Hey!" he protested, flailing wildly as he tried to stay afloat. "Calm down. They won't sting you if you don't touch them."

"But they're floating *towards* us!" I replied shrilly.

"Follow the other guys. As fast as you can. But be careful," he said. He began swimming to the right. He had strong, powerful strokes, and I struggled to keep up with him, but somehow I managed. We were slowly but steadily catching up to Savannah.

Then Ryan swore.

"What?" I asked, panicking. He let out a cry of pain, and terror shot through me.

"Little bugger stung me," he hissed, gripping his arm. I gasped in fear, as a jellyfish swam past.

"W-What do we do?" I asked, feeling tears welling in my eyes. "Oh my God, can you swim?"

"Get help," he said, gritting his teeth. I looked over at Savannah.

"Savannah!" I shrieked. She turned her head.

"Help!" I wailed. "Ryan got stung!"

Savannah called out to Alex, and the two of them headed back towards us. Ryan was cursing under his breath, and gripping his arm.

"Hold onto me," I insisted, wrapping his good arm around me to make sure he didn't float into any more jellyfish.

Alex and Savannah finally reached us.

"Let me," Alex said, taking his arm from me. He was a better swimmer than I, and he managed to support Ryan as they both struggled around the sea of jellyfish, and headed towards the shore.

By the time the shore came into view, there were a dozen staff members gathered there, as well as all the guests who were watching and helping people out of the water. Lifeboats littered the shoreline.

When our feet finally scraped the sandy shore, we staggered out of the water—exhausted, breathless, and drenched.

Escaping from a sinking cruise ship had *not* been on my bucket list.

Ryan collapsed on the beach, looking like he was in a *lot* of pain.

Courtney spotted us and came rushing over. Alex went to get help, while Savannah and I stayed at his side.

I fell to my knees. I didn't know exactly what jellyfish stings felt like, but I could tell that they were painful as hell.

"Ryan? Can you hear me?" I asked frantically.

Ryan opened his eyes and smiled weakly. "Loud and clear," he winced.

"Oh, good," I said quickly. I was panicking again. "Can you, like, maybe not die?"

"I don't plan on dying," he promised. "Not until I get another kiss from you, anyway."

I flushed red, and Savannah nudged my arm playfully.

"Now isn't the time to make jokes!" I scolded, whacking his arm. Then I gasped. "I'm sorry! Did I just hurt you more?"

"You couldn't hurt a fly," he teased weakly.

I resisted the urge to hit him again.

Alex brought over a staff member with a first aid kit who began to treat Ryan. I slipped my hand into his as they put vinegar on the sting. He was swearing again.

It almost felt ironic how all this had happened in one night. I had experienced all the things I'd been most afraid of—a cruise ship sinking, running into deadly sea creatures. . .

And Ryan getting hurt.

CHAPTER FOURTEEN

TAKING THE HIGH ROAD

As soon as it looked like no one else was hurt, and the staff deeply apologised for the ordeal, everyone headed back to their rooms.

I anxiously led Ryan back to our cabin. There were so many feelings going on inside me at that moment. I was absolutely *traumatised*, and worried about Ryan, and, most of all, exhausted. My clothes were soaked and cold, and the calmness I'd felt on the cruise had completely disappeared.

"I am so sorry," Ryan said, just before we reached the room.

"Why are *you* apologising?" I asked.

"Because that should *not* have happened on your first cruise," he replied. "I cannot believe it did."

"I kind of just want to forget about it," I said quietly, before heading inside. I hadn't realised it before, but I was shaking violently. I let Ryan use the bathroom first, to change and shower. He took a little longer due to his injury. As soon as he came out, I made a beeline for the bathroom, too cold to wait any longer.

Although the last thing I wanted to do was surround myself with more water, the warm shower did help wash away the salty feel of the ocean. I made sure to bathe myself in especially fruity scents to overpower the horrible stench of the sea.

When I emerged, Ryan was sitting on his bed looking gloomy.

"Does it hurt?" I asked gently.

"Yes," he replied. I hesitated, but then sat by him and wrapped an arm around his shoulder.

"I can't believe you got stung," I said, my voice shaking.

"It was heading for you, you know," he said quietly.

I froze.

"What?"

He turned to me. "That's why it stung me. I put my arm in the way so it wouldn't sting you," he said.

I was speechless. He'd done that for *me*?

"Why?" I whispered.

He gave me a look.

"Aubs," he said. "I was not about to let a jellyfish make your fear of the ocean even worse, certainly not after you had just escaped from a sinking cruise ship."

"But it *hurt* you," I said, my voice getting even weaker.

He fully turned towards me. "It's fine," he said. "We both made it back in one piece, after all."

I was silent for a few minutes. I didn't *feel* like I'd made it back in one piece. I felt like I'd been splintered into shards, and that all my emotions had separated, leaving me detached.

"You're shaking," he whispered finally.

"I can't stop," I replied, my voice breaking. Then I was crying and he was hugging me, even though his arm was in pain and he was probably the one who needed the hugging. He stroked my hair gently and pulled me into his chest so I had no choice but to inhale his scent—the soapy scent, the thing that was distinctly Ryan.

And it soothed me.

And then he started singing again. I tensed a little, remembering what had happened the last time he started singing. I wanted to pull away.

"Do you want me to stop?" he asked.

I thought about it.

"No," I said finally, sniffling. "Just don't kiss me."

"I won't," he promised. His voice was calming and lovely, and before long I finally stopped shaking, and was able to relax in his arms. When he noticed that, he stopped singing, and I thought he was going to let me go. But he didn't, so I stayed there in his embrace for a while longer.

"I'm surprised," he said finally.

"About what?" I asked quietly, breathing in his scent.

"You didn't completely melt down when the boat started sinking. You panicked, but you kept your wits about you. You were brave," he said. "I was thinking I'd have to carry you out princess-style or something."

"It's only because I was too busy trying to get off the boat to stop and cry about it," I replied. "In case you haven't noticed, I'm having my meltdown right now."

"And you have every right to have one. I'm just glad you chose now rather than then," he said.

I doubted if I'd ever go on a cruise again, or near the sea for that matter. After the jellyfish incident, that was the last thing I wanted.

I didn't want to leave his arms. I was afraid that if I did, all my thoughts and fears would come rushing back to me and I'd lose it again. I couldn't handle that right now.

"Can I sleep with you?" I whispered.

He tensed.

I blushed, realising how that must have sounded.

"I just meant . . . by your side," I said quickly.

"Do you trust me enough?" he asked softly. I looked up at his face. His blue eyes were intense and serious.

"You saved me from a jellyfish and helped me escape a cruise ship. I definitely trust you enough to sleep next to you," I said. He smiled a little, and reached over to pull back the covers.

I climbed into his bed, and his scent lingered faintly throughout his sheets. He reached over to switch off the light and climbed in next to me. I was facing him, and he stroked my hair softly.

A part of me was starting to wonder why he had teased me all those years. He didn't seem like the same Ryan who was capable of that anymore. He had changed right in front of my eyes.

I was tempted to ask right then, but I didn't know if I could handle it— not after everything that had happened. So I let it slip my mind for the time being.

And we drifted off to sleep in each other's arms.

~

When I awoke, it was because something was on top of me. My eyes opened and I saw an arm draped heavily over my waist, pulling me close. The early morning light was just visible behind the curtains.

I needed to roll over and stretch, but I was stuck and I didn't want to wake Ryan up. His breathing was steady and slow and soothing. I kind of wanted to run my hands through his soft looking dark hair, but I resisted the temptation. I wondered what time it was.

Carefully, and slowly, I slipped out from under Ryan's arm, and sat up. The alarm clock read 5:53 AM. I got out of bed and went over to the counter to make Ryan a cup of coffee. I felt like we were alternating now. Tomorrow he'd be making my coffee. And the next day I'd be making his.

I also didn't want him to use his injured arm if he didn't have to. That, and I felt like I owed him for saving me and letting me sleep in his bed and everything else.

When I'd finished making the coffee, the alarm clock read 6$_{AM}$. Ryan must've smelled the coffee brewing because he woke up.

I gently sat on the end of his bed, and, as he sat up, I passed him the mug. He gave me a smile.

"Is this going to be a thing?" he asked.

"I think so," I replied, smiling back. He took the cup and gave me a look of gratitude. He sipped it, then pulled a face.

"Did you put something in it?" he asked slowly, looking at it in disgust.

"Of course not!" I replied, worriedly. "Does it taste bad?"

Then he grinned and nudged me. "I'm just teasing. It's perfect."

I scowled at him, but I couldn't help breaking into a smile.

"Did you sleep okay with your arm?" I asked.

"Of course I did. You were with me," he replied. I flushed a little.

"I don't get it," I said quickly. "You've completely changed the way you act towards me. How is it that you are so nice to me now when you weren't before?"

"I still haven't told you why I was mean to you in the past," he said. "Are you ready to find out . . . or do you still have trouble believing things I say?"

I shook my head. "I want to know," I said. He put his mug down on the table and gave me a serious look.

"This is actually the most pathetic reason, but it's the truth," he said. "When I was younger I thought you were really cute. I wanted to talk to you, but I also thought you looked scary because of your hair."

I *knew* it was the hair! Didn't I say it?

He went on. "Every time I tried to approach you, I got intimidated. So eventually I started picking on you, trying to be tougher than you. I just wanted to get your attention, so you'd notice my existence, but I guess it all kind of went the wrong way, huh?"

"It sure did, Buddy," I said grimly.

"Well, once I started, I couldn't think of another way to get you to notice me, so I kept doing it. And then you started talking back to me, which I liked, but you were horrible. And since I always thought you were scary, I figured you'd always been like that. So I never really thought it was all my fault until you said it," he said. "I didn't realise how much I'd hurt you. I grew up under the impression that you were my bitchy next-door neighbour, but, in truth, it was all because of me. And I'm sorry. I really didn't mean for that to happen."

"Well, I guess you *were* just a kid," I said. I found myself believing him. It was the way he was looking at me that told me he was telling the truth—the sincere honesty in his eyes.

He went on. "I've kind of always had a crush on you. Even though you were mean to me. And then, when we went on this vacation, I saw your vulnerable side, and I took advantage of it because, for once, you *weren't* mean. You were *different*, and it made me wonder about you. If it hadn't been for your fear, I never would have seen you differently."

"So I guess my fear turned out to be a bit of a good thing," I said.

"More than a good thing," he said, tucking a strand of my red hair behind my ear. "Because now I'm sure of my feelings for you. I'm six feet under the sea and drowning when you're not with me. You're like a fiery storm, a beautiful hurricane. You have a temper that matches my own, and you make me realise when I'm going too far.

"You make me feel needed, and I know I need you. I feel like I'm only coming up for air when you're with me. And it leaves me breathless every time you leave."

Once again I was speechless, mostly because I never imagined anyone would feel that way about me.

I had no idea how to respond. All any guy had ever seemed to see in me was a short temper.

After a long pause, I said, "Ryan . . ." I trailed off. "I had no idea . . . about any of that. I didn't realise my looks could be the cause of our hatred." I smiled. "I was right about your flaw. You really *are* swayed too easily by looks."

He grinned for a few moments before speaking again. "Do you believe what I'm telling you?" he asked, suddenly looking worried.

"Yes. I do," I replied softly. "It should be hard for me to believe you, but, for some reason, I do."

"Then do you trust me enough to let me kiss you?" he whispered. "Because I kind of really want to."

"I think, from now on, you can kiss me all you like," I said with a smile.

He leaned in and brushed his lips against mine, cupping my face gently. Then he kissed me again, a little harder. It caused tingles and shivers to run down my arms, and soft, fuzzy feelings to sprout in my chest. It felt like tiny electric sparks shooting through my veins, and like a wave washing over me, erasing all the pain from the past. Our kiss eroded all the hatred between us, until all that was left were tiny, fizzy bubbles that left us both feeling giddy and ecstatic.

We finally stopped for air and he leaned his forehead against mine.

"I really am sorry about the past," he whispered.

"I forgive you," I replied, still a little breathless. He intertwined his fingers with mine and held me in his arms for a while. We sat there, and he rested his head on top of mine.

"I've been wanting to kiss you and hold you like this forever," he murmured into my hair.

When we finally pulled apart, I went to wash his coffee mug. He followed me to the mini fridge and started looking around inside.

"There isn't any ice," he frowned.

"Why do you need ice?" I asked.

"My arm is hurting a little," he replied.

"Well, we could go find some," I suggested.

236

We changed and headed outside. Instead of going to breakfast, I suggested we go to the Tiki Village. I was sure they'd have something there.

We went looking inside a store, and I found frozen juiceboxes in the freezer section.

"You could use this, and when it melts, you can drink it," I suggested.

Ryan agreed, so we grabbed two and headed for the register. It was crazy busy, with lots and lots of people shopping. I guessed the majority of these people were those who lived on the island, as tourists probably didn't have as much need to be grabbing a week's worth of food when the food hall was available.

"That's right," I overheard the checkout lady in our line saying to her customer. "The cruise ship *went down*. Yes! Someone sabotaged it!"

"No way!" the other lady was saying.

"The police arrived this morning to investigate," the checkout lady explained. "They had a team out on a boat, diving down to bring up whatever wreck-age they could. Looks like someone blew a hole in the side or something."

"How did someone manage to do *that*?" another customer asked, this time a man. "The security needs to be doing a better job when checking the luggage, by the sounds of it."

Ryan and I exchanged a glance. Perhaps what I'd overheard the staff saying last night had been right. It gave me all the more reason to stay away from boats, as far as I was concerned.

After we paid and walked out, Ryan held the juice box against his bandaged arm and sighed, look-ing relieved.

"So what should we do today?" he mused.

I gawked at him. "Are you crazy?" I protested. "You're in no shape for activities. You need to rest!"

"Aw, come on," he protested. "I don't want to sit around all day."

"Well, what do you suggest then?" I asked, rais-ing an eyebrow in challenge.

His gaze landed on something above my head. "How about that?" he asked.

I spun around to see what he was talking about, and looked up. My heart sank.

He was looking at the volcano. Mt. Kapua, to be exact.

It didn't erupt anymore, according to the island brochures, but I wasn't exactly jumping at the idea of hiking up a volcano, even if there was supposed to be a decent café waiting at the top.

"Um . . . anything else?" I asked nervously.

"Well, what else *can* we do?" he asked. "The volcano hike is challenging, but it doesn't involve water . . . and I hear the views are great from the top."

I grimaced. Well, at least he wasn't running off to go skydiving or anything like that. And, I had to admit, the idea of standing at the top and looking out at the beautiful view with Ryan sounded very romantic.

"Okay. Fine," I said, giving in. "We'll do the volcano hike."

~

Ryan said the hike would take about an hour and a half. The path up the mountain wound round and round a jungle of trees, all the way to the top where a café overlooked the islands. By the time we were ten minutes into walking, we'd already busted open our juice boxes and had started sucking what had melted out of them.

"Well, at least this way we can pace ourselves to stay hydrated," Ryan sighed, as he tried to get a few more drops out of his.

I was so glad it was still early morning. If it had been any later it would have been even hotter, and I already felt like I was melting.

I didn't think it could get worse.

But it did.

I heard a shrill cry from behind us, and spun around.

Courtney was racing up the path towards us, waving. We waited for her to catch up.

"Hey," she breathed, panting when she reached us. She leaned over and put her hands on her knees.

"What's up?" Ryan asked her.

"Well, I thought about taking a hike today after what happened last night," she said, still gasping for air. She straightened up a little. "And then I spotted you guys. We should all hike up together! What do you think?"

I honestly didn't want to, but what choice did we have? It wasn't like we could just tell her no when we were all headed the same direction anyway.

"Sure," I said. She grinned, and headed over to Ryan's other side.

"So, that was pretty scary last night, huh?" she said. The way she kept reminding me of what happened last night made me tense up again, and I shoved the memory straight out of my mind before I could start crying. It wasn't as easy as it sounded.

Courtney's eyes landed on Ryan's arm. "How's your sting?" she asked.

"It's better than yesterday," Ryan replied. Courtney rubbed his upper arm soothingly, like she was trying to be reassuring.

I felt that bitter taste return to my mouth as a twinge of jealousy rippled through me.

Why did something feel so off about this?

As we walked, Ryan and Courtney chatted, and I just listened to their conversation. Courtney went on and on about a lot of things. Her interests seemed to be a big topic for her, and I noticed she kept making excuses to touch Ryan in some way. Feeling annoyed, I reached out and took his hand in mine. He shot me a small smile and instantly squeezed my hand. Courtney watched us, getting the message. I gave her a warning glance, and she backed off a little.

When we reached the top of the hiking trail, the view really *was* breathtaking. There were blue skies and sea for as far as you could see, and all the islands were scattered along the water like little dollops of green.

The café was small, and I noticed a little house behind it. Whoever ran this place clearly had no intention of hiking up and down each day.

We headed inside, and I was blessed with cool air conditioning and the promise of a cold drink.

"I'll go get the orders," Ryan suggested. "Aubs, what do you want?"

"Something cold and caramel flavored," I replied. Caramel was my favourite flavor.

"I'll have the same," Courtney added. I fought the urge to narrow my eyes at her.

As Ryan went over to the counter to order, Courtney and I went and found a table for three. We sat facing each other, and I tried to keep my expression friendly. She drummed her fingers on the table's surface, looking around the shop and taking it all in. Then she turned to me.

"So, are you two a thing?" she asked finally.

"Yeah," I replied.

"But I thought you two hated each other," she frowned.

"Things changed," I said, to keep it simple. She nodded, but her eyes glinted dangerously. It was unnerving, to say the least.

When Ryan returned, I breathed a quiet sigh of relief. Courtney went back to smiling and, to my utter horror, flirting. Even with the knowledge that he was off limits, she was still trying to seduce him.

I glared at her, all friendliness gone. She caught sight of my expression and simply smiled innocently, before going back to touching his arm and comparing the size of his biceps to other guys she knew.

Worst of all, I couldn't tell what Ryan was thinking. He acknowledged everything she said, and made no attempts to ignore her or get her to stop. But he wasn't jumping at the attention, either.

Ryan had ordered Courtney and I a caramel milkshake, and a vanilla one for himself. I drained mine as fast as I could, eager to get out of there and away from the likes of Courtney. Who did she think she was stealing Savannah, and now trying to steal Ryan? And what was up with the whole innocent act?

It ground my gears to no end.

At one point, Courtney accidentally knocked a napkin off the table, and both she and Ryan reached for it. They head butted each other, and both shot back up, wincing.

"Sorry," Ryan said quickly. "Are you alright?"

"Ow," Courtney winced, rubbing her temple. Ryan reached out to touch her head, like he was going to pat it or something.

That was too much for me. "I'll be back," I muttered. I thought I was going to be sick, and this time seawater had nothing to do with it.

The bathrooms were empty, thank God. The moment I got in there, I hung my head over the sink and looked at myself in the mirror. I took a good, hard look.

Why was this upsetting me so much?

Courtney had *nothing* on Ryan. If Ryan was telling the truth about our past, then there was no reason to doubt how he felt about me. I'd chosen to trust him.

I couldn't let that trust waver now. I'd let down my walls, and let him into my life.

Ryan had said all those amazing things to me that morning. There had been such honesty in his words when he described how he truly felt. It was impossible to think that those had been lies. There was no way he could have been acting.

I took a deep breath to calm myself. With those comforting thoughts in mind, I headed back out into the café. I made my way towards the table, then froze in shock.

Because Ryan and Courtney were kissing.

CHAPTER FIFTEEN

TRUTH BE TOLD, I'M LYING

I didn't stop as I rushed out of the café, my vision blurred by hot tears.

I couldn't get the image out of my head. It was like it had been carved there. Courtney's hand behind Ryan's neck as she pulled him closer, their mouths pressed together.

Now I *really* wanted to vomit.

How could I have been so stupid, so horribly, utterly, easily deceived? Of *course* none of it had been true. Of course.

As I raced down the hill, stumbling and feeling the rush of my rapid descent, I let my choked sobs echo out through the trees. I eventually came to a stop, and collapsed in the middle of the path, shaking, and feeling weak.

I'd been betrayed. I'd been fooled. I'd let him get to me. I should *never* have trusted him. It had to have all been an act. I wouldn't have been surprised if Courtney and Ryan had a thing going on behind my back, like some huge joke that everyone else was in on. Let Aubany get close and then BAM, stab her in the heart.

From the start, I'd known better than to trust Ryan, but he'd burrowed his way under my skin and stuck himself to me like the salt in the air and the chlorine in my hair. He had known exactly how to get to me, and use my fears as a way of gaining my trust. And then, when he'd known I had completely fallen for him and let down my guard, he'd swept in for the kill. He threw a grenade and let it take me down in one hit, while he escaped with my trust and, undoubtedly, an enormous sense of satisfaction at his achievement.

His greatest achievement yet, I bet.

Getting me to fall for him.

If only I'd been strong enough to know I had been part of his game all along. That side of him would *never* truly change. He was Ryan Rupert, after all—the jerk, and my mortal enemy.

There was no way he'd ever fall for a weak girl like me.

When I finally had the strength to stand, I made my way down the rest of the mountain and headed straight for the cabins. My first thought was to pack up everything I owned and get my own room, but then I realised I couldn't afford my own room.

So my next thought was to call Savannah and ask if we could share. I called her, but she didn't answer.

Great.

I found myself wondering if she was in on it, too. She and Courtney were like two peas in a pod. Maybe they'd planned it. Savannah knew about my hatred for Ryan. Maybe she'd told Courtney, and they'd found a way to use it as my weakness. Maybe they all just wanted to ruin my life.

I was halfway through packing my suitcase, throwing clothes and toiletries in haphazardly, when Ryan walked in. He saw me packing my stuff.

"Whoa, what's going on?" he asked, looking confused.

I shot him an icy glare.

"Oh. I see. We're pretending to be clueless are we?" I spat angrily.

His eyes went wide with shock. "What are you talking about? What happened to you?" he asked, but I quickly cut in before he could continue.

"What did you *think* would happen?" I cried, throwing my hands up. "Did you think I'd hang around? Let you continue to manipulate me? Well, it's done. You did it, Ryan. You completely ruined me. All the trust I had in you is gone, and you've turned me into a pathetic . . . e-excuse for . . . for a human b-being," I began to sob. I threw down the shirt I was holding.

"Aubany . . . I'm lost," he said. "I thought you got sick and I couldn't find you . . . You didn't see . . . Did you see . . ." he trailed off, looking sheepish. He must have known exactly what I was mad about, but he was still refusing to mention it. He looked like he was dealing with some kind of wild animal—unsure how to approach, and terrified for his well-being

Well he *should* have been terrified, because I was *so* done, and he was going to hear everything I had to say about it before I walked away from him forever.

"Tell me, Ryan," I said slowly, sniffling. "Did you plan it? Was it all part of the game? To rip out my heart and tear it to shreds? Because you and Courtney did a really good job. A *really* good job. And you two are completely perfect for each other. So why don't you just go back to her and kiss *her* again instead of standing here and playing with my emotions!"

Hot, angry tears ran down my face. My voice was like sandpaper; I could hardly speak from being so choked up.

"Aubs, let me explain—" he protested, but I held up my hand.

"You don't have to explain a single thing," I seethed. "I get it. I'm weak, and pathetic, and she's pretty and talkative and showers you with compliments, which I imagine does wonders for your stupidly huge ego!" I shouted.

I slammed the suitcase shut, letting it fall from the bed, and smack on the ground. I dragged it along the floor and stormed past him.

"Aubs, *she* kissed *me*!" Ryan insisted, reaching over to grab my arm. I shook him off.

"It's too late, and I don't care anymore," I said angrily. I glared at him. "I will *never* trust you again, for as long as I live, and you could have all the excuses in the world and I still wouldn't care. You've hurt me for the last time, Rupert."

"Aubany," he said, pleading, but I was already marching out the door.

I didn't know where to go, but I needed to get off this part of the island, so I headed to Savannah's room, hoping that I'd run into her or that she'd answer her phone. I was still crying, and probably looked like a blubbering idiot.

I guess I'd been right when I said this would be the worst vacation ever.

~

When I got to Savannah's room, I sat outside with my luggage and tried to stop crying. I succeeded and managed to only sniffle occasionally. Most of the white-hot anger had gone, leaving behind a well of sadness in my chest, along with regret and self-pity.

A pair of footsteps approached me, and I looked up to see Alex.

"Aubany," he said, looking surprised. "What's wrong?"

"Nothing," I said bitterly, not wanting to share my day with him. "Do you know where Savannah is?"

"No, I've been trying to call her all day, but she isn't answering," Alex replied. "I've been by her room twice already. She's disappeared."

I grimaced. I bet she *was* in on it, and she and Courtney were off celebrating now. Maybe she'd followed us, wanting to watch as my heart was destroyed.

I was such a fool.

"Do you need somewhere to wait? You could come to my room. It has to be better than sitting out here in the heat," he said.

I shook my head. "No, it's okay," I said quietly. I was about to give him my best *I'm totally fine* smile when my phone went off. I really didn't want to look at it, half afraid that it might be Ryan. But then Alex's phone went off, too. I pulled mine out as he checked his.

Savannah had texted us both the exact same message.

I think I figured something out about the cruise last night. Meet me at Palm Cove.

I frowned and met Alex's gaze.

"That's the place with the hammock, right?" I asked. Alex nodded. I got to my feet, deciding to leave my luggage in Alex's room, which was just down the hall.

We then headed to Palm Cove.

When we got there, it was deserted.

"Where the heck is she?" I asked, frowning. Was this some kind of joke? Could it be another prank? Was Alex in on the whole thing, too?

I wasn't hanging around to find out.

"I'm leaving," I said, turning to head back. Screw Savannah. I'd sleep on a bench somewhere, or under a few palm trees on the beach.

"Wait!" Alex called. "What if she's hiding? Maybe she doesn't want to be found."

I snorted. "Why would she be hiding?" I asked, but then I stopped.

Even the crew had known someone had caused the hole in the ship. Maybe Savannah knew *who* it was. Maybe she was scared they'd stop her from telling others the truth.

If so, maybe she *was* hiding. And maybe she *wasn't* against me.

I saw someone coming around the bend, but my heart sank and twisted in pain when I saw who it was.

Ryan.

He spotted me and slowed in his tracks. Then he eyed Alex, and a frown crossed his face.

"What's going on?" he asked slowly.

"What are *you* doing here?" I seethed angrily. I hoped that, for just a moment, he experienced the same horrible feelings I had when I saw him with Courtney. He shot me an annoyed look.

"I got a text from Savannah asking me to come here," he replied, in a matter-of-fact voice. I sighed and turned away from him. I looked around, and then noticed someone hiding in the bushes.

"There," I said, pointing.

Savannah was beckoning us over. We hurried to her.

"What is going on?" Alex asked, when he reached her. She hushed us, looking terrified.

"Were you followed?" she whispered.

An uneasy feeling developed in my chest.

"No," I said slowly.

Savannah breathed a sigh of relief. "I know who sabotaged the cruise, and I know why," Savannah said, looking at me. "Courtney did. She did it because she saw you and Ryan together."

Hot anger flared through me. That was *it*.

"Oh no, don't you even start with this," I said angrily. "It's all about *Courtney*, isn't it? Well, she already succeeded in ruining me, so why don't you just stop? You think she'd sabotage a cruise ship because of a stupid date? That's crazy! And I don't believe a word of it!"

"Aubany!" Savannah protested, looking anxious, but I stormed off again. Ryan and Savannah were calling after me as I raced away.

They were *all* in on it. All of them.

As I rounded the bend, and headed back past the pools, I ran into the one person I *really* didn't want to see.

"Oh. Hello, Aubany," Courtney said with a smile.

"Don't talk to me," I snapped angrily.

257

She ignored me. "You wouldn't know where Ryan is, would you?" she asked, playing with a strand of her hair.

"Oh yeah, I do. He's back at Palm Cove. Why don't you go *make out* or something? Make some more plans to ruin my life," I spat angrily.

"Oh, good idea. Maybe I will," she sang.

I gritted my teeth.

"I don't know what your problem is, or what you have against me, but you should know that I'm not falling for any more of your stupid tricks," I said. "I know you and Savannah have teamed up behind my back, and I know you're trying to make it seem like the cruise ship going down was your fault. I don't know what your motive is—maybe you're hoping it'll send me running back to Ryan, so you can rip the rug out from under me again. But it doesn't matter because I will *not* let you trick me."

She narrowed her eyes. "What gave you *that* idea? Do you really think I'm capable of taking down a cruise ship on my own?"

I frowned. She seemed kind of defensive about it.

"That's what Savannah said, but I know you guys are lying," I said finally. It was weird how she was acting like she didn't know what Savannah had said, like she wasn't in on it at all. She'd been so transparent and obvious when hitting on Ryan, I wondered why she didn't just own up to this as well—unless it really *had* been her. . . but that was impossible, and crazy, and *stupid*.

"How very interesting," she said finally, before heading off in the direction I'd come from.

I suddenly had a very uneasy feeling.

~

I spent the rest of the day avoiding Ryan and the others, hanging out near the beaches and just walking, meandering, trying to make myself untraceable. I'd even turned off my phone. Then, later that night, I went to fetch my bags from Alex's room. He shot a million questions at me but I ignored all of them, asking him to leave me be.

Without any explanation as to where I was headed, I made my way to a beach across the island, far away from Ryan and Savannah and anyone else who had hurt me.

There was no bench or hammock around, and I wasn't exactly the outdoorsy type who could fashion a tent out of a few palm tree leaves, so I settled in the sand against the trunk of a palm tree and decided to call it a night.

It kind of sucked being curled up in the sand, and I really needed to shower. I was using my suitcase as a pillow, but it was hard and uncomfortable.

Geez, and I though puking in a public bathroom had been my worst moment. If only my past self could see me now. I'd tell her to run far, far away before she fell for Ryan's tricks and charms.

Just when I felt I was finally drifting off to sleep, I heard a scream. I sat up and looked toward the sound, only to see a figure fall from the rocky cliff nearby, and land on the rocks below. My eyes widened in shock.

I jumped up and raced over, my heart pounding in my chest. I couldn't *believe* what I'd just seen—it seemed so surreal and out of place that I had to stop and question if maybe I *had* fallen asleep and was currently dreaming. But of course, if I'd been asleep, I probably wouldn't be feeling the sand getting kicked up into my shoes and the cold night air.

I saw someone moving in the darkness up on the cliff, a shadow. As they scurried away, I realised that whomever had fallen had been *pushed* by someone!

I scrambled along the rocks and found the body. I stifled a gasp when I saw a tangle of blonde hair.

It was Savannah.

CHAPTER SIXTEEN

LEAVE ME BREATHLESS

The first thing I did was check if Savannah was breathing. She was alive, thank God. Her arm was twisted at a funny angle, and she was pretty banged up.

Then I turned on my phone and call Reception for help, telling them I'd seen someone push my friend. I ignored all the missed calls and texts that rushed into my inbox from Ryan, a result of me having my phone off all day.

Luckily, Savannah had fallen into a gap between the rocks and landed mostly on the sand.

She had been *seriously* lucky.

Suddenly, I knew she hadn't been against me after all. Her terror from earlier had been real. There was no way this could be part of the act. No one would go so far as to put their lives in danger just to play a prank on me.

Savannah hadn't been working with Courtney after all.

My mind was racing as I waited for help. If Courtney was the only one behind this, maybe she *had* kissed Ryan, which meant Ryan might've been telling the truth.

I had refused to believe him. I'd said such horrible things to him.

I hadn't stuck around when I saw them kissing. If I hadn't jumped to conclusions and run off, maybe I'd have seen what happened *after* the kiss. If Ryan was telling the truth, I would have seen him push her away. And now that I thought about it, her hand *was* behind his neck, and maybe she was using it to hold him in place.

I mentally cursed myself for being such an idiot.

Here we were, on an island, with someone who actually went so far as to try and hurt my friend and split Ryan and me up. It made me think about what

Savannah had said about the cruise. If all of that was true, then Courtney really *could've* been responsible for taking down the cruise ship. It appeared she was *capable* of doing such a thing after all. And if the reason really had been my relationship with Ryan, then all of her flirting and the kiss made perfect sense.

Help finally arrived, and I followed them as they carried Savannah back towards Reception on a stretcher.

Maybe I should have been more worried about her, but I was still processing what Courtney had done. Tearing Ryan and me apart—and nearly killing Savannah, for that matter—was probably child's play compared to taking down a cruise ship.

Just how far did she intend to go, and why? What was the deal with me and Ryan? What was driving her to act in such a crazed manner?

~

It was a while before I was able to see Savannah. I had to answer a lot of questions while I waited. They took her to a medical room behind Reception.

She had been knocked unconscious, and had a few minor injuries and a broken arm, but, apart from that, she was okay. I waited by her side until she woke up.

"Aubany?" she said, opening her eyes.

I gave her a small smile. "Hey," I said. "How are you feeling?"

"Sleepy," she said. That was probably the morphine. "What happened?"

"You were pushed off a cliff, and I found you," I explained. "I think it was Courtney." I added.

"I don't remember it," she muttered, looking pained. Her face was scrunched up like she was trying to remember.

"Take it easy," I said slowly, and she stopped straining herself. "I'm sorry, by the way. About earlier today. Some things happened, and—"

"Ryan explained it," she cut in. "I can understand what you were thinking. I promise, I'm *not* working with Courtney."

"And I know that now," I said. It kind of sucked how it had taken Savannah almost getting killed for me to realise it, though.

"Well, good. I hope you also know that it was Courtney who kissed Ryan too. He looked miserable as he explained it. He was saying how he'd never be able to win you back again because of all your trust issues from the past. He looked kind of heartbroken."

I winced, feeling a stab of guilt.

"I was going to try and talk some sense into you, but I couldn't find you all day," she added.

"I was avoiding everyone," I replied. "I'll have more faith in you guys from now on. This is a scary situation. We can't afford to be fighting."

"I agree. I've already told the staff what I think Courtney did to the cruise ship, and they checked her room but all her stuff was gone," Savannah said. "I don't really think they believed me, though."

"I'm not surprised. Even I didn't believe it," I replied. "But, clearly, if she pushed you, she's still here on the island. Which means she must be hiding out somewhere," I said. Suddenly, the idea of sleeping under a palm tree wasn't as appealing, not with the knowledge that Courtney was running around.

Savannah was looking drowsy.

"I should let you rest," I said finally. I stood up and bid her goodnight as I left.

I headed back to the beach, but I had no intention of staying. I simply gathered my luggage and headed back to Sea Spray Beach.

Back to Ryan.

I felt so guilty. I'd let my emotions get the better of me, and now things had gone to shit again.

When I stopped outside the room, I realised I didn't have my key card. In the rush to leave earlier, I'd left it behind.

I raised my hand and knocked on the door. I waited.

It wasn't a long wait, but it sure felt like one.

When the door swung open, and his piercing blue gaze met mine, I almost melted into a puddle.

Ryan simply stared, not showing any emotions.

"You've been ignoring me," he said finally. I nodded, not trusting myself to speak.

"I was *worried*, you know," he added, a little icily. "I didn't know where you'd gone."

I bit my lip. "Savannah was almost killed," I said quietly. He fell silent, staring in confusion, like those words didn't make any sense in his brain.

"What?" he said finally.

"I found her. I was sleeping under a palm tree on the beach and I saw her get pushed off a cliff," I said.

He frowned.

"You were sleeping under a *palm tree?*" he asked, then he shook his head. "Wait, what happened to Savannah?"

"She's okay. She woke up, but she doesn't remember anything. But when it happened, it made me realise that you guys were telling the truth, and I was just being paranoid."

"So . . . you know it was *Courtney* who kissed *me?*" Ryan said slowly. "Because I would *never*—"

"I'm really sorry," I blurted out. "I should have had more faith in you. You even confessed all that amazing stuff to me, and I just threw it all back in your face."

"I don't blame you for doing so," Ryan said quietly. "If I were in your shoes, I'd probably have done the same thing."

"Will you forgive me?" I asked.

His expression softened.

"Are you kidding me?" he asked, smiling. "I should be the one saying that. For making you doubt me."

All I wanted was to hug him. Luckily, he was already reaching over to do just that. Being in his arms again made all the insecurities I'd created in my mind wash away. It pulled all my emotions back to me like a current, which made me want to laugh and bawl my eyes out at the same time.

"Aubs, I really thought I lost you," he murmured, running his hand up and down my back over and over. "I didn't know how I was going to get you back."

He pulled me into the room as I reached out to drag in my suitcase. I dropped it on the floor as he shut the door behind us.

And then he had me pressed against the wall, breathing in my scent, holding me in his embrace. "I can't stand the thought of you slipping through my fingers again," he whispered.

"I'm not going anywhere," I promised. His intense gaze was driving me a little crazy—in a good way. I hadn't realised how much I wanted him around me. I'd been so focused on the thought of him betraying me that I'd ignored the raw pain I felt in his absence.

He pressed his lips to mine. His kiss was soft and gentle, like he was afraid I might yell at him again. His fear of losing me was evident in his touch. He was treating me delicately, as though I was fragile, like he was afraid to cause another fight.

I knew I could trust him now, and I knew that kiss with Courtney had meant nothing. I didn't want him to fear losing me, I wanted him to have me, because my heart had entangled itself in a world of Ryan, and it was too late to escape. The feeling was was like seaweed rooting me in place, keeping me in this new underwater world that frightened and fascinated me at the same time. As much as I was afraid of getting hurt, I was prepared to stay. And, now that I could admit to myself how much I wanted to be with him, that feeling of trust got stronger with every moment I spent in his arms. The fears that had restricted my heart floated away like air bubbles.

I held onto him tightly, daring him to show his true feelings. He studied me intently, and I kissed his jawline, trying to coax out the Ryan who was hiding behind those feelings of fear.

"I'm not going anywhere," I repeated, a little more firmly. I could tell he understood. He fervently kissed my lips, my nose, my neck, making me sigh. I'd never felt this way before—no one had ever looked at me, or touched me, like this. For the first time ever, I had someone who *wanted* me, who made me lose my breath as he kissed me.

He guided me off the wall, towards the bed.

"Wait," I said softly. He stopped in his tracks.

"I'm all sandy from the beach, and I need to shower," I said. As much as I hated to stop him, I knew I wouldn't feel comfortable until I got rid of the icky feeling of dirt covering me.

"Okay," he said, though he seemed pained to lose me for even a brief moment. He traced my arms gently with his fingertips, before kissing my forehead and letting me go.

I went to my suitcase, grabbed a set of pajamas and went to the bathroom. When I got in, I realised I'd grabbed my pretty ones, the satin ones with the lacy trim. It hadn't been intentional.

I quickly stripped down and covered myself in the soap's scent of oranges and citrus, happy to wash away all the nastiness of the day—from the hike to the fight with Ryan to finding Savannah.

It was towards the end of the shower a feeling of nervousness came over me. Don't get me wrong—I *wanted* to go back to Ryan. But the way he'd been

kissing me . . . I couldn't help but feel like it was lead-
ing to something much bigger than anything I'd ever
experienced, and I wasn't sure if I was ready for that.
Two days ago, I hadn't had a *clue* what I wanted. And
now, I'd only *just* come to terms with how I felt about
Ryan.

Ryan, he . . . well, he was certainly more experienced than I. And although I had an intense curiosity
for what he could do to me, I was also terrified of
stumbling even farther into this unknown territory.
Love . . . and *sex* . . . it had never been a *huge* factor
in my life until now. And I honestly hadn't thought
much about when and how all these first experiences
would occur. Now, they were flying by so fast I
barely had time to check them off my bucket list.
What if I wasn't good enough for him? And how did
someone open up to another person that way? How
did someone *give* themselves over, in body and soul,
and trust that the other person wasn't taking advantage of them?

As I stepped out of the shower and dried off, I tried to calm myself. I changed into my pajamas, which felt smooth on my damp skin, and I looked myself in the mirror. *This* was the person he was kissing. *This* was whom he'd chosen, out of *all* the girls on this island, and all the girls in *Tallahassee*, for that matter. Wasn't that reason enough to trust him? After today . . . after everything he'd said to me . . . maybe I just needed to take a leap of faith.

I opened the door to our room.

One look at Ryan, and I just *knew* everything was going to be okay. All the insecurities faded once more.

He was sitting on his bed, and without even asking, I went straight to him and into his arms. His response was just as natural. He pulled me under the sheets and continued to kiss me, like I hadn't even left.

"I like these," he whispered, running his hands along the silky material of my pajamas. His touch made me feel like I was alight and glowing. He trailed hot kisses down my neck, and I had to admit how much I liked being bundled under the sheets with him in my arms.

I ran my fingers through his hair, feeling its softness. His eyes spoke a thousand words, telling me how much he liked that I was there, and how scared he was to lose me, and all the things he'd like to do if my pajamas were lying on the floor right now . . .

But I didn't let it go that far, because I knew I *definitely* wasn't ready for that yet.

Instead, he pulled me tight against him and we fell asleep in each other's arms, murmuring soft whispers of never letting go again.

~

We both woke up later than usual, after our emotionally exhausting day and night. The first thing Ryan did was make me a coffee.

While he was off showering, I drank the coffee, then got changed. I planned to go visit Savannah again. We needed to figure out what we were going to do about Courtney—and fast, before she struck again. The hotel staff were looking for her, but until they found her, we needed to make sure we were all safe.

When Ryan returned, he wrapped his arms around me and nuzzled his head into the crook of my neck.

"I need to go visit my parents today," he said, in his usual soft voice. "You can come if you want, but you don't have to."

I shook my head. "I'm going to see Savannah. But I'll meet you back here." He nodded, then kissed my cheek before standing to leave. I watched him go.

Warm feelings fluttered through my chest.

Speaking of parents, I needed to call mine. I grabbed my phone and dialled my Dad, waiting until he picked up.

"Hey, Sweetie," he said.

"How's Mom?" I asked.

"She's getting better, they think. We should be able to come home soon, which means you can come home too, if you want to. In maybe two weeks or so.

Your Mom can get the rest of her treatment at the hospitals in Florida."

I felt a feeling of disappointment settle in me. Not about my Mom getting better, but about leaving.

"Actually Dad, it's okay. I'm enjoying myself here," I replied.

"Really?" he sounded surprised.

"Really," I confirmed. "Can I talk to Mom?"

He put her on.

"Aubany," she said brightly. "How are you?"

I practically beamed. "Mom . . . Ryan is amazing."

"*What*? I thought you guys hated each other," she said.

"No, quite the opposite," I replied. "He's been helping me with my fear of the sea." I wanted to tell her about him kissing me . . . but not yet. Soon though.

"Well, that's good, honey. I'm glad you're both getting along," she said.

I was quiet for a moment, before saying what was on my mind.

"I want to stay," I told her. "I mean, I'm really glad you're getting better. Like, *incredibly* glad. And I can't wait to come home and see you again . . . but I actually like it here. And I want to spend the entire vacation with Ryan."

"Really?" she said, sounding amused. "Well, that I'm glad about. I think it's good that you're both having a good time, and you *should* stay there. If it's what you want, then I don't want to stop you from having a vacation."

"Are you sure?" I asked gently. I really wanted Mom's honest approval on this. She was in need, after all, and if she wanted me home, then . . . I'd go.

"I'm *positive*," she said finally, and I exhaled a breath I hadn't realised I'd been holding. "I'll let you know when the doctors give me the clear to go home. Just remember . . . you *can* come home whenever you want to if you change your mind. Otherwise, I'll see you when you get back."

Those words echoed strongly through my mind. *I'll see you when you get back.*

As in, for real. As in, she *was* going to come home.

I couldn't help but smile at that thought.

"I'll talk to you again soon. I have to go in for treatment now," Mom said.

"Okay," I said. "Bye. I love you."

After I'd hung up, I headed out the door.

~

Savannah looked way better today than she had last night. She smiled brightly when I walked in to visit her.

"They're saying I should be able to leave by this afternoon," she said. "I'm glad. I'm sick of this bed," she added.

I laughed.

"Well, that's good news! Now, what are we going to do about Courtney?" I asked. "We can't wait for her to try and attack one of us again."

"I know, but what *can* we do?" Savannah asked. "We don't have any proof she pushed me. It was too dark for you to see. We're only going off what we know about her kissing Ryan and sabotaging the cruise ship, and even *that* hasn't been proven yet."

"How *did* you know she sabotaged it?" I asked, suddenly curious.

"Well, she was asking me a bunch of questions beforehand about you and Ryan. Personal stuff. And I remember seeing her heading below deck at one point during the cruise. I was only assuming, but from the looks she was giving you two all night, I'd put any amount of money on it being her."

"Wait, she was giving us *looks*?" I asked, my stomach twisting.

Savannah nodded.

"Really nasty stares," she replied. "Alex saw them too."

It made sense that it was Courtney who sabotaged the ship, especially since she pushed Savannah. I mean, why else would she try and kill her, other than to shut her up? Savannah was the one who figured it out, after all.

Then, my blood ran cold.

I'd·been the one who told Courtney that Savannah knew, back when I was angry and thought they were working together.

It was *my* fault that Savannah was here right now.

"Aubany, what's wrong?" Savannah asked, watching me. "You look pale."

"I . . . I have to go," I said quickly, standing up and rushing out. I couldn't be around her right now. *I'd* nearly killed Savannah! If I hadn't been so blinded by anger, I wouldn't have endangered her!

She'd been scared, that was why she'd hidden away, so that she could tell us what she knew without *being* overheard. She was terrified that Courtney would find out!

I felt sick.

I headed out of reception and past the pools, heading for Palm Cove. I needed to be alone for a while.

When I got there, it was deserted as usual.

I walked up to the hammock and went to sit in it, but I jumped back when I realised someone was already in there.

Courtney.

"Oh, hi Aubany!" she said, smiling as innocently as usual. I took a few steps back from her and she swung herself off the hammock. Why was she always popping up when I least expected it?

Suddenly, my anger overtook me.

"I . . . I know what you did," I said quickly. "You pushed Savannah, didn't you?"

Courtney narrowed her eyes at me.

"Why would you say that?" she asked slowly. She took a step towards me, making me back away even farther. I froze as my feet touched something cold and wet—the ocean.

As Courtney walked towards me, ocean waves lapped at my feet.

I swallowed hard. "You sabotaged the ship . . . and you tried to kill Savannah. You tried to make me hate Ryan. But why?"

"Why indeed?" she mused, looking pleased. "Too bad you'll never live to find out."

And with that, she lunged at me.

I gasped and stumbled backwards, farther into the ocean. She grabbed my arm and covered my mouth with her other hand, pushing me down into the water. I screamed, but it was muffled by her hand.

I frantically kicked, trying to push her off me. The ocean waves rushed over my head, blinding me and stinging my eyes. I shut them tightly and tried to focus on pushing Courtney off me. My heart was pounding, and my lungs were begging for air.

I was suffocating. Drowning. *Dying*.

Salty water filled my nose, burning the back of my throat. I continued to fight, but then decided to try and reserve my energy as much as possible. I let myself go limp, hoping Courtney would think I was dead, hoping she'd let go so I could come up for air.

My lungs were bursting, my thoughts clouding. I felt her hands release me, and I was free. I opened my eyes, but it was too late. My vision was already turning black, and the glittering sun rays in the water above me were slowly fading to nothing at all.

CHAPTER SEVENTEEN

MUSICAL DISTRACTIONS

Air tore through my lungs. My body slowly began to kick back into action. My lungs were screaming at me to breathe.

I was trying to, but I couldn't.

Breathe.

My eyes wouldn't open.

"Breathe, Aubany!"

I felt something against my mouth. I suddenly gasped, choking up water. I doubled over and coughed, gasping for air, gripping the sand beneath me. I gulped, trying to inhale as much as I could. My lungs were hurting. I swallowed mouthfuls of air.

I became aware that I was back on the beach.

"Jesus, Aubs," I heard Ryan's voice say. It sounded strained. I looked up and saw him kneeling next to me. "Thank flipping hell I took that CPR course last year," he said, looking relieved.

"Where's . . . Courtney," I choked, still trying to get my breathing to return to normal.

"She's gone. I pulled her off you. It was either save you or grab her, and I'd choose you any day," he said, stroking my cheek.

"She tried to kill me," I realised. Ryan looked grim.

"Savannah called me, saying you ran out on her. She said something was wrong with you, so I came looking for you. I thought you might come here to be alone . . . but then I saw you being *drowned* . . ."

"Shhh," I said. "I'm okay now. How many times have you saved me so far?" I asked.

"Too many," he agreed. "What happened? Why did you run off?"

"I told Courtney what Savannah knew. Back when I was angry, without realising what she'd do. It's my fault she almost died," I said. "I felt so bad, I came here. But then I found Courtney, and I confronted her . . . which was stupid to do alone. I didn't think she'd try and kill me, too . . . but of course she would."

"Well, this has gone on long enough," Ryan said. "From now on, no one is going anywhere without a buddy. Savannah has Alex, and you have me. If we run into Courtney again, we're not going to confront her. We're going to get a staff member right away."

I nodded, shivering. My clothes were soaked again. Why did I even bother wearing clothes? I should've just walked around in my bathing suit, since it was clear I was constantly coming in contact with water.

"We should go back to the room so you can change," Ryan suggested. Shivering, I agreed.

~

After we'd been back to the room and I'd changed my clothes, I couldn't sit still. I kept pacing, unable to let myself rest, because if I rested for just *one* second all I could focus on was Courtney.

"Maybe you should sit down," Ryan suggested, watching me anxiously. "We can watch a movie?"

"No way. If I just sit around here, I'll keep wondering where Courtney is and freaking out. I need a distraction."

"You've already told me *I'm* a good distraction," he purred, giving me a look that made me feel weak.

"Agreed, but I'm not in the mood for *that* kind of distraction," I replied. I had, after all, nearly died.

Suddenly, Ryan's eyes lit up. "I just thought of something perfect!" he exclaimed. He grabbed my hand, snatched up my key card and his wallet, and almost dragged me out of the room.

"What is it? Where are we going?" I asked, stumbling after him.

He winked at me. "It's a surprise," he told me.

When we reached the Tiki Village, Ryan walked along at a quick pace.

"Are we going *shopping*?" I asked. "Is this what you're so excited about?"

"Come on . . . come on . . ." he kept muttering to himself, looking hurriedly in each window.

Suddenly he stopped and grinned.

"Ha! What are the chances?" he said. "Come on!" He raced inside one of the stores.

I looked up and saw it was a music shop. Well, kind of. They had little bongo drums and stuff in the window, and I saw ukuleles hanging on the walls. That's what Ryan went over to. I followed him.

"What's your favourite colour, Aubs?" he asked.

"Blue," I replied. He grabbed the blue one and took it to the counter.

"Why are you buying a ukulele?" I asked him.

"I'm going to teach you how to play one," he replied. "That's got to be distracting enough, right? I mean, learning music is hard."

I realised what a brilliant idea that was.

"What if I suck?" I asked. since I already sucked at paddling and getting into hammocks.

"Then I'll just play you songs all day and sing to you," he said, smiling.

We took our new ukulele down to the boardwalk, near Savannah's room. We found a bench under a palm tree, with the waves below us, and sat down.

"Pick a song, Aubs," he said.

"Any song?" I asked. "But don't we need sheet music or something?"

"I can't read sheet music," he admitted. "But, I can figure out any song's notes in a few minutes. That's how I learned."

"How?" I asked. I had no idea he was so musically talented. He plucked one of the strings, and a sound rang out.

"You listen to the sounds, and match them. It takes a bit of practice," he said. "Here, this one is a G."

He put his arms around me so we were both holding the ukulele, and he placed my fingers on the right strings. I strummed a chord.

"What songs do you know?" I asked.

"Tons," he replied.

"Let me guess, are they all Jonas Brothers?" I asked teasingly.

"Maybe," he said, winking. I laughed.

"Will you play me something?" I asked. A smile played on his lips.

"Sure," he said. He took the ukulele from me and began strumming. I recognised the tune immediately.

"Wait . . ." I said slowly. "That's my *favourite* song."

"Well, I had a feeling since I can always hear it playing from your room," he replied. "So I decided to learn it because of that."

It was "Wonderwall", by Oasis.

"Do you want me to teach it to you?" he asked. I nodded, smiling.

He showed me the basic chords for the melody, one by one. G, then A#, then F, then D#. And, as I strummed them, he sang to me. His voice was so nice, and when he was singing my favourite song . . . well . . . it was *super* nice, and very romantic.

We stayed there all day, until our fingers hurt from strumming and the sun had started to set. We ended up going back to the room. When we got there, a look of annoyance crossed Ryan's face.

"Damn it," he muttered, checking his pockets.

"What?" I asked worriedly.

"I left my key card in my parents' room when I came back to find you," he said. "I'll have to go get it tomorrow."

"Why don't you just go get it now?" I asked.

"I can't be bothered right now," he said.

I shrugged and opened the door to let us in. Once inside, Ryan placed the ukulele on the counter and I sat down on my bed.

My thoughts began to take over again.

I had nearly *died* today, but I didn't feel any different. I'd always thought that an experience like that would leave more of a mark on a person, but I'd spent the entire day singing pop songs and strumming a ukulele, and only now was I realising how crazy that seemed.

It was because I was so weak that my life had been in danger. If I was stronger, I would have been able to push Courtney off me. My day would've been better spent training or working out, not singing.

Ryan noticed my pained expression and came over.

"You alright?" he asked gently.

"Ryan . . . why do you like me?" I asked suddenly. "I am so incredibly weak. You're right. You've saved my ass so many times. *Too* many times, and it's because I didn't have the strength to protect myself, when I should."

"Whoa, hold on," Ryan said, kneeling in front of me and taking my hands in his. "You are *not* weak, Aubs," he said.

I raised an eyebrow. "Are you kidding me? I couldn't even push another girl off me, and because of it I nearly *drowned*!"

"You don't have physical strength, that's true," he said. "But you have strength inside of you. In your heart. You have the determination to try your hardest, and get through things."

I snorted. "Ryan, I spend half my time whining and crying whenever I'm faced with one of my fears."

"Which is a natural reaction to fear," he replied. "And it's part of dealing with it. Aubs, you are *incredible*. Yes, like everyone, you have some bad qualities, but you have just as many, if not more, good qualities to make up for them."

"Like what?"

"Well, for one, you're an amazing dancer," he said. "And you make really good coffee." He smiled.

"That's not going to save my life," I pointed out.

"You're also smart, and bold enough to voice your true opinions when it matters," he said.

I smiled a little, and he leaned in closer.

"Plus, you're beautiful, and you're pretty good at distracting me."

"I thought *you* were the distracting one," I said.

"We're both pretty distracting. A good match, huh?"

Now I couldn't help but smile properly. He leaned in and kissed me gently.

"How exactly am I distracting?" I asked softly, my hands wrapping around his neck as we fell back onto the bed.

"You're being distracting right now," he breathed. "The way you're looking at me."

He kissed just under my ear, and I let out a sigh.

"And when you make noises like that," he added in a whisper.

I tangled my fingers in his hair as he continued to kiss me. My hands found their way to his chest, then to his waist, and he sucked in a breath as they traced the top of his shorts. My eyes flicked to his for a second, and he returned my gaze.

Slowly, unsure and cautious, I slipped my hands up under his shirt.

Now, I'd seen Ryan without a shirt before, but that had been back when he wasn't exactly my favourite person. *Now*, though, it had a whole new effect on me.

He let me slip the shirt over his head, and I kind of just stared for a few moments. Ryan had abs, and they were so *defined* and *sexy*. I traced my fingers along them, and he inhaled sharply. His eyes darkened a little with something that sent a tiny thrill through me, like a flicker of electricity.

Then all of a sudden, the door swung open.

I gasped, my first thoughts flying to Courtney. Was she here? Had she found our room and broken in?

Then Renee appeared in the doorway, and boy was she shocked to find us together on the bed in such a position.

"I . . . wow, um . . ." she said, staring. "I found your key card Ryan and . . . I was just returning it . . . when exactly did *this* start?"

My face was probably as red as my hair at that moment.

"It's not how it looks!" I protested quickly.

She raised an eyebrow.

"Then how exactly is it?" she asked.

Ryan was less embarrassed than me. He looked a little awkward and sheepish, but, apart from that it seemed more like he was trying not to laugh at the situation more than anything. A smile kept tugging at the corners of his mouth.

"Well," he began, facing his Mom. "When a boy and a girl love each other *very* much—"

"*Okay*, I don't want to know!" Renee cried, as I gawked at him and whacked him on the shoulder.

"Aubany," Renee said quickly. "Can I have a word with you in private?"

"Sure," I said, a little reluctantly. Something told me this was going to be very awkward.

We went outside and Renee turned to face me. I was probably still blushing.

"So . . . you and my son are . . . what are you exactly?" she asked. She looked like she was trying to wrap her head around it.

"Well . . ." I began. I wasn't exactly sure myself. We weren't *dating*. At least, not officially. But we'd definitely established very strong feelings.

"We like each other," I said finally.

Renee nodded slowly.

"Okay," she said. "Well, I can't always be here obviously. And I have a feeling you wouldn't want me here anyway. But I do expect you two to act responsibly, seeing as you're sharing a bedroom. Wherever you take your relationship is up to you, of course. But take my advice and don't rush it."

"I understand," I said quickly. "And I wouldn't have let him go too far. Or have gone too far myself."

"Right," she said, looking almost embarrassed. "Well, now that that's cleared up . . . take this," she said, handing me the key card. I took it and thanked her.

"And I'll just . . . get out of your hair," she said, nodding as she turned to leave. "Oh, wait. Aubany," she said quickly, looking back. She paused, like she was trying to form her words.

Finally, she said,

"I'm glad he fell for you, of all people. You're very mature for your age, and he could use someone like you in his life."

"Thanks," I said slowly, feeling a little proud.

She turned and headed off, and I went back inside.

To my disappointment, Ryan had put his shirt back on.

He looked up as I walked in. "Did she get in your face?" he asked.

"No, nothing like that," I said quickly. "She just wanted to know what was going on and . . . where it was going."

"Right," Ryan said, nodding. "Talk about a mood killer."

I let out a laugh. He grinned at me.

"So, you're not worried about Courtney anymore, right?" he asked.

I grimaced. "I am, but I can deal with it. What you said earlier definitely helped."

"I'm glad, because she's not worth worrying over," he said, crossing over to me. "The staff are going to find her, don't you worry. And until then, I will keep you safe. She won't hurt you again, as long as I'm here."

He pulled me towards him and hugged me tightly. Then he added softly, "And I'm not going anywhere."

CHAPTER EIGHTEEN

FRIENDS CLOSE, ENEMIES CLOSER

The next few days passed without any issues, which was both a relief and a concern. For all we knew, Courtney could have disappeared from the island altogether. Or, she could still be lurking, plotting how to attack us again.

Either way, we didn't know, so we stuck to our room just as a precaution.

Ryan almost went crazy with boredom, but somehow he managed. I probably helped with that—if he'd been on his own he'd truly have nothing to occupy him, and movies could only entertain you for so long.

We didn't hear anything about Courtney until about a week later, when Ryan snapped and insisted we go out for *just* an hour.

We ended up going to the Tiki Village, and walking along the boardwalk to the stall to get some ice cream.

"What flavour to you want?" Ryan asked me.

"Caramel. Always caramel," I replied, grinning. He got himself a vanilla one, and we went off together, happily eating our ice creams.

As we headed back through the village, I spotted a newspaper stand outside the grocery store.

On the front of the newspaper was a picture of Courtney.

"Ryan," I said, grabbing his arm. I led him over and made him hold my ice cream so I could grab the newspaper. I unfolded it, and read the headline.

I almost dropped it.

"Oh, my God," I breathed, my voice laced with fear.

The headline read *Asylum Patient Still Missing*.

Courtney had escaped from a mental institution! She was actually, legitimately *crazy*.

P.S.Malcolm

"You've got to be kidding me," Ryan said, looking shocked. "We've been stuck on an island with an asylum escapee? And she's targeting *us*?"

"Ryan, we have to do something," I said fearfully. "We haven't seen her for days. We have to tell someone she was here!"

"I know," he said gravely. "Come on. Let's take this back to the hotel reception."

We paid for the paper and headed over. The reception staff brought over the manager, and we showed him the headline. We went on to explain everything about Courtney, how she tried to drown me, and how we suspected she'd pushed our friend and sabotaged the cruise ship. It was a little hard to make those last arguments sound convincing, seeing as we didn't have any proof.

The manager told us they'd been searching but hadn't seen Courtney, and Reception said she'd checked out late last week. They said they'd keep an eye out just in case, but that we shouldn't worry too much about her.

As we made our way back to our room, an uneasy silence settled between us.

"Do you think she's really gone?" I asked quietly.

"I don't know, Aubs," Ryan replied. He was about to say more when we turned the corner and spotted Savannah outside our room, her eyes red like she'd been crying.

"Savannah? What's wrong?" I asked, rushing over to her. She looked at me.

"Aubany!" she breathed. She hugged me tightly. "Aubany, she has Alex!"

"What?" I asked. "*Courtney*?"

"I found this," Savannah sniffled, handing me a note. I took it and read it.

I have Alex, and I will not reveal his location. If you wish to see him again, unharmed, you will have Ryan meet me at Palm Cove tonight at midnight. He will come alone, and no staff will be alerted, or I will not hesitate to severely harm Alex.

You know I am capable of doing so.

Should Ryan not show up, Alex will be killed and you will follow, then Aubany. Think carefully before deciding, Savannah. The clock is ticking.

-C.

"The clock is ticking?" I asked. My blood ran cold. "You don't think she has a bomb, do you?"

"Don't be ridiculous," Ryan said, taking the note and reading it. "She may have taken down a cruise ship, but there's no way she could get a bomb onto the island."

"Maybe she built one?" I asked. "I mean, she *did* blow a hole in the cruise ship."

"Again, we don't *know* that for sure," Ryan pointed out. "We know she was behind the attack, but we don't know *how* she pulled it off. I think it's just an expression, Aubs," Ryan said.

His words didn't reassure me in the slightest.

Savannah gave us a pleading look. "You guys *have* to help me," she begged.

"How? Do you want me to turn myself over to her?" Ryan asked.

"No!" both of us cried.

I feared for Ryan. What would she do to him? He couldn't go.

"There has to be something else we can do," Savannah said quickly, her expression pale. "But we can't get the staff involved. Or anyone else. It's too dangerous. Alex will get hurt."

"I think we *should* get the staff involved. They have more experience than us," Ryan replied.

"No, Savannah's right," I said quickly. "It's too much of a risk. We have to figure this out on our own."

"I'm not afraid of Courtney," Ryan said quickly. "I can go. I'll get Alex back to you, Savannah."

"*No*, Ryan!" I pleaded. "What if she hurts you?"

"In case you haven't noticed, I'm the only one who hasn't been attacked yet," Ryan said.

"Exactly!" I cried. Wasn't that all the more reason *not* to go?

"Well, what if she doesn't want to attack me? She kissed *me*. She sabotaged the cruise ship because you and I were together. She wants *me* to meet her, and she didn't say *anything* in the note about killing me. I don't think she intends to hurt me."

"Then what does she intend on doing?" Savannah asked fearfully.

"She's crazy," Ryan said, "so I don't have a clue what she's thinking. But I can handle her. I'll return with Alex, I promise."

I wanted to protest, to keep him safe. But he had such a determined look in his eyes, I knew that he wasn't going to change his mind.

"Ryan, you are the best," Savannah sniffled, looking grateful. "Aubany is so lucky to have you. Just be careful. If you get hurt because of me, I'll feel awful."

"I'll be fine," he promised us. He gave me a reassuring look, but all I could do was shake my head.

~

We spent the rest of the day in our room. Savanah, Ryan and I tried to keep our minds off Alex, but we couldn't. We were too worried about him to do anything else.

I sat with Savannah, hugging her, and Ryan flipped through the TV channels, trying to distract himself. When nightfall came, Savannah told us she was going to go back to her room to shower.

"You can come right back after if you want," I offered. She shook her head.

"I need some time alone. Just, call me when you find him," she said.

We promised to, and she left.

I glanced at Ryan, who wasn't showing any signs of fear, if he had any.

"Maybe you should get some sleep," I offered. "I'll wake you when it's time to leave."

"I'm fine," he promised.

"Ryan . . ." I trailed off. "Please. It would put me at ease to know you aren't too tired to fight her if you need to."

P.S.Malcolm

He frowned. "Aubs," he said softly. He reached over and took my hand. "Do you really want me to?"

I nodded. He sighed.

"Okay. If it makes you feel better, I will," he said. He gave my hand a squeeze, and went over to his bed to lie down.

I sat by his side and ran my fingers through his hair until his breathing became steady and slow. I waited until it was almost time.

"I'm sorry," I whispered ever so quietly. I kissed his forehead and got to my feet. As quietly as I could, I threw on my jacket and laced up my sneakers. There was *no* way I was going to let Courtney have her way with Ryan. I was going to face her, and bring Alex back myself. If I lost Ryan, I didn't know what I'd do.

I tiptoed to the door and opened it. I was halfway out when someone grabbed my hand, pulling me back into the room.

"What are you *doing*?" Ryan asked harshly. I bit back the urge to curse.

"I can't let you go, Ryan," I said, turning to him. He looked angry.

"Aubs, you are *not* going to face Courtney. Last time you saw her, she almost killed you!"

"Well what if she tries to kill *you*?" I protested. "Why does she want *you*, Ryan? What is she going to do? I can't sit here and wait for you, not knowing!"

"So you just figured you'd go in my place? Betray *my* trust?" he asked, looking wounded. "You wanted me to prove myself to you so that you'd trust me. I need to be able to trust you too, Aubs. Why would you sneak off like this?"

"I don't want you to get hurt!" I cried. His expression softened.

"Aubs," he said gently. He pulled me closer and hugged me. I buried my head in his chest and hugged him back tightly.

"I'm sorry," he whispered. "But I can't let you face Courtney."

He suddenly bent down and picked me up.

"Wait! What are you doing?" I asked frantically. He carried me to the bathroom. I tried pushing away from him, but he was too strong.

"Ryan, let go of me! Put me down!" I insisted. He placed me on the bathroom floor, his expression pained, and shut the door.

I grabbed the handle and tried to open it, but it wouldn't budge. I heard the sound of something moving, and realised he was pushing furniture in front of the door to keep me in there.

"Ryan! Let me out of here!" I screamed, banging on the door. "Stop! You can't go! Please!" Tears sprang to my eyes and I pounded harder.

"Aubs, I'll be back," he said, his voice muffled from behind the door.

"No! Don't you dare leave!" I screamed. "Don't leave me here! Ryan! Ryan, come *back*!"

I heard the front door open and close.

"Ryan!" I sobbed. I slumped against the door and sank to the floor, crying. I couldn't believe he'd locked me in! I needed to get out! I needed to stop him before Courtney did something horrible!

My hand flew to my pocket, remembering my phone. I quickly dialled Savannah's number.

"Aubany!" she said. "Did you find him?"

"Savannah, I need help!" I said, trying to keep my voice even enough to be understood. "Ryan locked me in the bathroom. You have to get into my room and get me out! Right now!"

"How? I don't have your key card!" she protested.

"Go find a staff member with a master card," I said, remembering back to my first day when I'd walked into the wrong room. "Please hurry!"

She hung up and I waited. I was impatient. I paced. I stared at myself in the mirror. My appearance was ragged and my face was tear-stained. I debated just breaking the window open, but it was too small for me to crawl through anyway, and I probably would've cut myself trying.

I fumed about Ryan. I cried again. Then I got mad at myself for crying and being weak and useless. I planned exactly what I'd say to Ryan when I saw him again. I'd yell at him for locking me up, tell him how much he meant to me, yell at him again for scaring me, and then maybe kiss him if I felt nice enough.

Finally, I heard noises outside and the door to the room opening. There were voices, and the sound of furniture being pushed aside, and then the bathroom door flung open. Savannah stood there with a staff member.

"Thank God," I breathed, hugging her. I looked over to the staff member. "Thank you," I added.

"Is there anything else I can help you with?" she asked, eyeing me suspiciously like she wanted an explanation for why I was locked up in my own hotel room.

"It's okay. I'm fine," I reassured her. Once she had gone, I grabbed my key card and dragged Savannah out the door. "We have to get to Palm Cove."

We sprinted across the island as fast as we could. It was nearing midnight now.

Ryan had gone early, but he was probably waiting there for Courtney.

I didn't want to endanger Alex, so I led Savannah along the top of the hillside that concealed Palm Cove. We hid in the bushes as we crept along, occasionally peering out.

Below us, Palm Cove was completely empty, except for one figure standing alone.

Ryan.

I was tempted to race down there, but it was too close to midnight. Courtney could show up at any second.

We waited, and finally a boat came into view on the water. It was small and quiet. We were able to make out Courtney in the darkness, but there was no sign of Alex.

"Where's Alex?" Savannah whispered fearfully.

"What if this is a trap?" I realised, my blood turning ice cold. "What if she left Alex wherever she's been hiding, and this was just an attempt to get Ryan alone?"

"She's a liar!" Savannah said angrily. She went to move, but I grabbed her.

"No. She still has Alex, so she's still capable of hurting him if we show ourselves. She isn't a liar. She just worded the note in a way that made us assume she'd hand him over right away."

She was *clever*.

Courtney got off the boat, and went over to talk to Ryan. They were too far away for us to hear them. I saw Ryan stepping back, shaking his head at first, and then freezing when Courtney spoke again. Then, very slowly, he took a step forward. He folded his arms and had a pained expression on his face.

Then I saw him walk toward the boat, Courtney following behind.

"What is he doing?" I whispered fearfully.

He was *leaving* me! He would have just left me in that bathroom had I not found a way out myself! A flicker of annoyance went through me.

But mostly, I felt fear.

Not too long ago, I would have worried that Ryan was leaving with Courtney because they had a thing going on. But I knew better now. I trusted Ryan with all my heart, and I knew he was mine, so I wasn't scared he was leaving me for Courtney. I knew there had to be another reason or threat forcing him to do so. And I knew I wouldn't rest until I found out where they were headed.

As I watched the boat disappear from view, I vowed that I would be the one to save him this time.

CHAPTER NINETEEN

FINDING RYAN RUPERT

We couldn't rent a boat so late at night, so we weren't able to follow Courtney. We did find a brochure though, which had a map of the island in it. We highlighted the most likely places she could be hiding.

We searched the main island all night, but were unsuccessful. We didn't stop until we'd literally driven ourselves to the point where we couldn't keep our eyes open any longer. We went back to my room and slept in the early hours of the morning. Savannah took my bed, and I took Ryan's. His scent soothed me, reassuring me that I would find him.

When I woke the next morning, I made myself a coffee. A pang of sadness went through me when I saw Ryan's cup sitting alone in the sink.

I crossed off all the areas on the main island we'd already searched. The rainforest would be a good place to hide, and we hadn't searched there yet. We'd already searched the Tiki Village, all the beaches, and the pools.

"I have an idea," I told Savannah, as she took a seat next to me on the bed. "I'll check the rainforest. I've been on the hike, so I'm less likely to get lost. You check the hike up to Mt. Kapua. There isn't a lot of forest to hide in on the way there, but you never know. Up on the top, there might be something. If we don't find anything, we'll meet back here and check the golf course on Pualani Island."

We set off. I headed to the rainforest and followed the trail until I was a fair distance in. Keeping an eye out for good hiding spots, I trudged along. I strayed from the path a few times to investigate other areas, but mainly stayed on it to avoid getting lost. Eventually, I found myself at the centre of the forest, where the trail ended. A giant waterhole was there, and I snooped around for caves and other hidden spots, but found nothing.

~

When I got back to the room I had to wait another half hour before Savannah returned.

When she arrived, she shook her head, so we headed over to Pualani Island and walked around the edge of it.

The golf course took up most of the space, and there was no way you could hide inside it. Besides, people went through there all the time.

We checked the edges of the island to see if there were hiding spots, but there weren't any. Disappointed and worn out, we headed back to the room to order food.

"We should check the other islands tomorrow," I said.

If I tried to do any more walking at that point, I would surely collapse. My fear for Ryan and Alex was intense, and I was worried about what Courtney

319

was doing to them, but I wasn't going to be any use if I was too tired to fight her.

We ordered pizza because it was easier, and once again, I was reminded of Ryan. That was the night he first kissed me.

A wave of sadness washed over me.

I wanted him safe. I *knew* he shouldn't have gone to meet her. I had tried to stop him, but I wasn't strong enough to fight *him*, let alone her.

After Savannah and I had eaten and showered, we went to bed again. I hugged Ryan's pillow against my chest and drifted off to sleep, only to wake hours later, screaming. I was having a nightmare.

Savannah jolted up from her bed, her eyes on me. When she realised I was okay, she breathed a sigh of relief and came over to hug me.

I was breathing heavily, covered in sweat. I clutched the pillow a little tighter and sobbed quietly, leaning into her.

Her comfort was different from Ryan's. Savannah made me feel cared for, but Ryan made me feel safe. He made me forget all my troubles completely. Savannah smelt faintly of Taylor Swift perfume and other musky scents, while Ryan smelt like fresh soap.

I couldn't shake that terrifying feeling that lingers after you have a nightmare. It was like a cold fear had taken hold of my heart. It felt like ice-cold water suffocating me, and even the warmth of Savannah's hugging couldn't make it go away.

I was so scared for Ryan. I hated not knowing Courtney's intentions, her capabilities. I hated being so useless and weak. If only I could find him. If only I didn't doubt my ability to rescue him.

I didn't end up falling asleep again, so I decided to go for a walk to clear my head. Savannah went back to sleep, so I wrote her a note to tell her where I was, and snuck out quietly.

As my feet touched the cement pavement outside, I heard a crumpling sound. I looked down and saw a folded piece of paper wedged under the door. My heart skipped a beat as I bent down to pick it up.

It was another note from Courtney.

Dearest Aubany,

My plans are not progressing the way I wanted them to. Your dearly beloved Ryan refuses to cooperate with me unless he gets to see you one last time. As much as it pains me to allow you two to be reunited, I feel this is the only way I will get him to do my bidding.

I am offering you a deal. I will give you a hint regarding my location. If you are smart enough to figure out our whereabouts, then you pass my test and earn the right to see him again.

If you do find us, you are to come alone, without a boat or any other kind of transport. If I see anything of the like, Alex will die immediately.

If you should arrive safely, I will trade Alex for you, and release him unharmed. You will take his place. After that, Ryan will do exactly as I say, or you will be harmed.

As for my hint, well, it's a secret.

Good luck, Aubany. You have until tomorrow, midnight.

As I read it, I felt fear wash over me. What the hell? How was I supposed to find them when she hadn't even given me the hint?

Panic overwhelmed me. How was I supposed to do this? I knew I *had* to do this. If I didn't, Savannah wouldn't be reunited with Alex, and I wouldn't be reunited with Ryan. I debated whether to tell her about the note, then decided not to. I had to go alone, and I knew she'd freak out if she knew I was going after Courtney. She'd insist on coming with me.

It was early morning now. The sun was beginning to rise, and I only had so much time to figure out where Courtney was holding Ryan and Alex. I scanned the note again, trying to see if there was a hidden clue I hadn't spotted before. But I found nothing.

Annoyed, I folded the note and pocketed it, before heading back into my cabin. We had to search

323

the other islands today. Maybe we'd find them by chance.

~

Later that day, Savannah took a dinghy over to the Lanikai Islands. She wasn't as terrified of island hopping as I was, so she figured she'd be better off alone.

I went to Tarang Island, which was smaller and took far less time to search. It was mostly covered in jungle, as well as some accommodations and the lagoon. After two hours of walking, I'd circled the entire island and found nothing.

The fear within me grew stronger as Courtney's new deadline ticked closer. I took a boat back to the main island, heading to the Tiki Village, where Savannah and I had decided to meet up.

When I got there, I stopped outside a building that I'd never bothered to look at before. It was a museum. Every other time I'd been to the Tiki Village I'd only gone in the shops. But now, as I looked at the museum in front of me, an idea formed in my head. Maybe *this* would provide some clues. After all, it contained all of the island's history.

I went inside and saw lots of small exhibits that talked about how the islands were formed and founded. I wandered through, heading to the back of the room where a giant, birds'-eye view photograph of all the islands was displayed. It was dated fairly recently, and it included every detail of the islands as seen from the air. It took up an entire wall, so you could clearly see every building.

I looked down at my brochure, which contained a drawn copy of the photo, but with coloured lines and symbols to mark each place and path. The brochure version was smaller than the photograph, and when I looked up, I noticed a tiny cluster of islands on the far right that *wasn't* included in the brochure.

I frowned, and read the sign below the picture for more information.

Originally, Nula Island was one large island, but over time parts of it were submerged in ocean water, to form smaller islands. One of these islands was not included as part of the holiday attraction, as it broke off into such tiny clusters that the founders were sure they would eventually go underwater. This part of the island was left unnamed, but is still reachable for exploration. Many of the island's staff refer to this part of the island as the Secret Islands, as many tourists are not aware of its existence.

My note. The hint said *it's a secret*.

She really *did* give me a legitimate hint! That *had* to be where they were. Where *else* would they be hiding, and how else could they have avoided being found by the staff for so long?

I smiled smugly.

I may not have been strong, but Ryan was right when he said I was smart and determined. If I hadn't been so driven to search for him, I might never have walked into the museum and found my answer!

I took note of the islands' location. It was right off the coast of Palm Cove. I rushed out of the museum. I had to get over there *now*.

When I stepped into the bright sunlight again, I remembered Savannah. If I left her, she might freak out. But if I told her, she'd want to come along. How did I do this without making her panic?

I then thought of a brilliant idea. I texted her, and told her I'd gotten sick from boating over to Tarang Island, and that I needed time to recover in my room. I told her I'd text her again when I felt better.

Once I'd done that, I went back to my room to put on my bathing suit. Courtney had warned me not to use a boat, so I'd have to swim. I left my phone on the counter so it wouldn't get damaged.

The very idea of swimming in the sea made my stomach squirm. After the jellyfish incident, the thought of it was more than a little unappealing. But I had no choice. I had to save Ryan, so I had to face my fears.

When I was ready, I dashed out the door towards Palm Cove.

CHAPTER TWENTY

KILLER INSTINCTS

Palm Cove was empty, as usual. I walked up to the water and gingerly nudged it with my toe. I was terrified. I had no idea how long I'd have to swim for, or if I could even make it to the island without drowning from exhaustion.

My thoughts reminded me of Ryan's jellyfish sting, of the entire sea full of jellyfish. I bit back a whimper.

No. I had to be strong. I had to just forget about all of that and concentrate on getting there alive. I thought about all the things Ryan had told me as I waded into the water.

"It's just like a swimming pool," I told myself, repeating his words. I thought about the time I went diving and remembered how beautiful it had been.

The cold water lapped at my face as waves came rolling past me. The salt water near my nose reminded me of almost drowning, and I gasped.

Take a deep breath, I told myself. Ryan needed me. I had to swim.

I began pushing my way through the water, trying not to think about the salt or the creatures that might find me. I focused on Ryan's face and kept reminding myself that he needed my help. I was the *only* one who could help him now.

After a while, my strength began to fade, fast. My arms ached and the tide kept pushing me back to shore, despite my swimming as hard as I could.

I'd only been in the water for about ten minutes when something brushed my ankle. I screamed and splashed frantically, panic taking over.

"Oh, God!" I wailed. I was going to die!

I then noticed a tiny fish darting past me, just as terrified by my outburst as I was. I breathed a shaky sigh of relief and continued swimming.

330

Half an hour later, my arms were hurting and I was paddling along weakly, too tired to go any faster. I eventually came to a stop and floated on my back, just trying to stay above water. A wave splashed over my face, making me cough and sputter.

I gasped for air, half crying, half fuming. Up ahead I could see the island on the horizon, but it was still too far away to make out the details.

Still, I was closer than before!

A new surge of determination shot through me, and I started pushing myself towards it as fast as I could. I wasn't going to die. I was going to make it.

I *had* to make it.

I then noticed something approaching me. A boat was coming my way, and Courtney's familiar gaze met mine as she rowed. I glared back at her. Here I was, paddling over to her stupid hiding spot like some pathetic weakling, while she cruised over in a rowboat. From the smile on her face, she seemed to be thinking the same thing when she came to a stop in front of me.

"So, you figured it out. I have to admit, you're smarter than you look," she sneered.

"Did you row all the way out here just to watch me struggle through the water?" I asked bitterly.

"No," she said. She offered me her hand.

"I was going to give you a lift. I'm impressed that you managed to make it this far on your own, what with your fear of the sea and all."

The last thing I wanted to do was take Courtney's hand and give her the satisfaction of knowing I needed her help, but I felt so tired from swimming that I honestly didn't know if I *could* have made it the rest of the way on my own, so reluctantly, I grabbed her hand and clambered into the boat. I was breathing heavily, and collapsed on the floor of the boat, trying to avoid her gaze as she smugly began rowing back to the island.

By the time we got there, I'd recovered enough energy to stand on my own. The island was overgrown with trees and deserted.

332

"Follow me, and *don't* try anything," Courtney said, climbing out of the boat. She pulled it ashore and headed into the forest. I followed her cautiously into the overgrowth, heading up a hill at a steady pace. While the plants weren't nearly as bad as the ocean, having the branches constantly hit me in my face got annoying as I pushed my way through the forest. Not surprisingly, Courtney didn't bother holding them back for me.

We came to a clearing, surrounded on all sides by forest. I spotted Alex and Ryan tied to the same tree. My blood boiled.

I did *not* like seeing Ryan tied up like that.

"You said you'd let Alex go," I told Courtney. She smiled.

"You're right. I did," she said slowly. She brought a knife out from the pocket of her shorts, and my eyes widened in fear. Why did she have *that*?

For a moment, I was fearful that she was going to go back on her word, but she crossed over to them and cut the ropes. Alex and Ryan stepped away from the tree.

Immediately, they both began to head for me, but Courtney stopped them, waving the knife in front of their eyes.

"Alex can take the boat back. I have another one ready," she said. Her eyes flicked to me.

"Aubany, step back against that tree. Don't try and run off with him, or I will cut Ryan."

I backed against the tree she pointed to. Ryan's eyes briefly met mine and he seemed annoyed. I couldn't understand why.

Alex slowly walked across the clearing, shooting me a thankful look. When he got closer, he muttered in my direction, "I'm bringing back help."

I nodded slightly. He disappeared into the forest. Courtney dragged Ryan over to me. His proximity was driving me crazy. I just wanted to hug him, but I didn't dare with Courtney waving the knife around. She stopped a few yards from me.

"You two get one minute," she decided, stepping back from us. Ryan tackled me into a hug, burying his face in my hair, and breathing in my scent. I held him tightly.

"Why did you come?" he whispered, sounding angry.

"Of *course* I came. I've spent the past two days searching for you," I replied. He looked me in the eye.

"Now *you're* in danger. God, I can't believe you were stupid enough to come after me," he said. A stab of hurt shot through me as he said those words.

"Are you kidding me?" I breathed angrily. "I just swam through God knows how much ocean water to get to you. I walked every inch of the islands looking for you, and you have the nerve to tell me I'm *stupid*?"

"Aubs, she's tricking you," he said firmly. "She has this crazy plan—"

"Time's up!" Courtney snapped. She seized Ryan and pulled him away from me, holding the knife at me to warn me not to follow. "Now, Aubany, I want you to be a dear and just stay where you are. I'm going to tie you up."

I glared at her.

"Are you kidding me?" I asked. "I'm not letting you tie me up!"

She raised an eyebrow and brought the knife up to Ryan's throat, her grip still firm on his arm.

He attempted to twist out of her grasp, but she only inched the knife closer to his throat, stopping him. Then, she shot me a smug look. "I suggest you do exactly as I say, or Ryan will be leaving here wounded."

"Leaving?" I asked. "Where are you going?"

"Ryan and I are going away from here, to be together," she said. "We're *meant* to be together. You're just the pathetic weakling that got in our way."

I stared at her in confusion. She was *insane*. Ryan didn't look too thrilled by what she was saying either.

"You do realise Alex is bringing back help," I said, trying to stall her.

"It doesn't matter," Courtney said. "By the time he reaches the island, finds help, and gets back here, Ryan and I will be long gone . . . and you will be long *dead*."

Ryan tensed, and I fought the urge to whimper. Instead, I shot Courtney my best glare and said, "You've already tried to kill me once. It didn't quite work out. What makes you think you can kill me this time?"

Courtney was now tying Ryan against the tree again.

"Ryan can't save you this time," she said. "Once you're out of the way, everything will fall into place. Won't it, Honey?" she asked Ryan.

He glared at her. "Don't. Touch. Her," he said, his voice deadly quiet.

He gave me a look that told me to run, but there was no way I could leave when she'd threatened to hurt him, so I stayed where I was, frantically trying to think of a plan.

Courtney secured a knot, then gathered another rope and headed towards me. Ryan was giving me a pleading look now, mouthing *run.*

I stood my ground.

Her eyes had a frightening expression. She looked crazed, determined, and terrifying. She grabbed my arm and held me against the tree.

I narrowed my eyes at her.

I didn't have physical strength, no. But I had something better.

I swung my head forward as hard as I could, head-butting her. She let out a pained cry, clutching her head.

My own head throbbed, which told me it hadn't been the best idea.

I kicked, striking her in the leg. She stumbled, losing her balance.

I snatched the knife out of her hands and ducked under her arm, sprinting towards Ryan. I quickly began cutting the ropes as fast as I could.

"Aubs, forget about me. Run!" he insisted.

338

"I'm not leaving you," I replied. I had not swum all the way out there just to leave him behind.

The ropes were thick, so they took a little time to cut through. When they finally broke, Ryan yelled, "Watch out!"

He pulled me out of the way just as Courtney lunged for me, and the movement made me lose grasp of the knife. It thudded on the ground.

Courtney eyed it hungrily, and, since I was too scared to try and snatch it back, I threw dirt up in her eyes instead and grabbed Ryan's hand.

"Come on!" I said, dragging him through the forest. We sprinted hand in hand, as fast as we could. We ducked under branches and ferns, barrelling our way through plants, stumbling over roots and fallen branches.

"Left! Left!" he said quickly, steering me down one path that had popped up all of a sudden. We raced along.

"Is she following?" I gasped fearfully.

"Yes. Get to the boat!" he insisted.

Apparently, he knew where the boat was, because he was directing me where to go. He helped me slide down a hill, and dragged me through more forest. Finally, I could see the beach up ahead.

"The motor takes a minute to turn on properly," Ryan said to me.

"How do you know?" I asked.

"I tried escaping before. Anyway, you need to distract Courtney until I can turn it on," Ryan said.

"You want us to split up?" I cried, fearfully.

"It's the only way," he said.

"Okay. I can do it," I said, more to myself than him.

As soon as we reached the beach, he let go of my hand and sprinted over to a boat nearby. I quickly took a right and ran. I glanced back and saw that Courtney was chasing me, oblivious to Ryan.

I darted into the trees again, intending to circle my way back to Ryan, but as I ran back into the forest, I met a wall of rock.

We'd raced downhill as we were escaping, and I didn't realise that was the only way to get through the forest.

I came to a stop, breathing heavily. If I ran back towards Ryan, I'd surely run into Courtney. But if I went the other way, it would take ages before I got back to him, and I was already out of breath.

Before I could make a decision, I heard the sounds of branches moving and twigs snapping, and Courtney grabbed me from behind.

"Get off me!" I yelled, trying to escape her grip. She shoved me forward against the rock, and I gasped as she twisted my arm back, and held the knife against my throat.

"Ryan. Is. *Mine*," she hissed angrily.

"Even if you kill me, Ryan will *never* go with you," I replied firmly. "The only reason he hasn't tried to take you down yet is because he doesn't want me to get hurt."

"That's a lie!" she cried.

"Is it?" I challenged. "Why don't you ask him for yourself?"

She narrowed her eyes at me. "Fine," she said. "I will. Let's go."

She held my hands behind my back and marched me towards the beach. As Ryan came into view, I heard the boat motor roar to life. He looked up and spotted me. When he saw I'd been captured, he grimaced.

"Let go of her, Courtney!" he said.

"Why? Don't you want her dead?" she asked. "She's the only thing standing in the way of our future!"

"Yeah, see, here's the thing," Ryan said, stepping out of the boat. "I don't *want* a future with you, Courtney. I don't understand what caused you to think I did, but I only have one future in mind. And it's with Aubs."

I smiled a little.

I felt Courtney tense behind me. For a moment, all I could hear were the ocean waves breaking on the shore beside us.

"You're lying," she said quietly.

"No," Ryan said. "I'm sorry, Courtney. I'm not."

She let go of my hands. I realised she was shaking. I tentatively stepped towards Ryan, away from her, just watching.

"Don't you *remember* me, Ryan?" she whispered finally, looking devastated. I slowly glanced at Ryan, frowning, but he looked just as confused. He shook his head slightly.

Suddenly, Courtney let out an angry cry and lunged towards Ryan. I watched, wide-eyed, as she lifted the knife and angled it towards him. I gasped, realising what she was about to do.

"Stop!" I screamed, darting in front of him. I felt the knife slice into me, and I let out a choked cry. Sudden pain spread over my stomach, but I was too shocked to cry or do anything but stare at Courtney.

Her expression suddenly turned to panic, as she realised what she tried to do to Ryan. I

slowly collapsed into the sand, curling up, clutching my stomach.

"Oh my God, Aubany," Ryan said, his voice filled with panic.

I saw Courtney back away in fear, and then she suddenly ran for the boat. I heard it leaving, but I was in too much pain to look.

Gentle hands took hold of me, and I realised I was in Ryan's arms.

"Aubs?" he whispered shakily. I smiled weakly at him.

"I'm still mad at you for locking me in the bathroom," I told him slowly.

He didn't laugh.

"Aubs, stay with me," he said. I'd never seen Ryan panic so much before. That alone told me the wound was bad.

He ripped off his shirt and, for a second, I couldn't comprehend what he was doing, but then he scrunched it up and pressed it to my wound. Cradling me, he let his head rest on mine.

"I can't believe you took a knife for me," he whispered.

"Ryan . . . will you sing to me?" I asked softly. I wanted to hear something calming, and his voice always soothed me.

"Of course I will, Aubs," he whispered. His voice cracked and was kind of choked up as he began singing.

I recognised the song immediately and laughed, which was a bad move. A sharp pain in my side turned my laugh into a cough.

"You're singing Miley Cyrus?" I asked in disbelief, smiling weakly. What *was* it with his obsession with Disney?

"It's the first thing that popped into my head," he replied, with a shaky laugh. His smile faded away as his eyes welled up with tears.

I felt safe and warm in his arms.

"Aubs . . . I haven't told you this yet but . . . I *love* you," he whispered, caressing my cheek. "Like, a lot."

A warm feeling spread across my chest.

"And I really don't want you to die on me right now," he added, his voice cracking. "So . . . maybe. . . don't close your eyes like that . . ."

My eyes felt heavy and they kept fluttering shut. I could still hear his voice, but I couldn't make out the words.

Before I knew it, my world fell into blackness as the pain in my side numbed into nothing.

CHAPTER TWENTY ONE

ANCHORED

When my eyes opened again, I became aware of a dull ache in my lower stomach, and someone holding my hand. I groggily blinked, trying to adjust to the lights.

"Aubs," a soft voice said. I turned my head and saw Ryan seated on my left. He broke into a relieved smile and buried his head against my hand.

"Thank flipping hell," he breathed. He kissed my hand gently and looked at me again.

"What happened?" I asked. "Where are we?"

"We're in the medical room behind Reception," Ryan said gently. "Alex found us. He brought staff over to rescue us."

I remembered Courtney, being on the island, and being stabbed. I winced at the memory.

"Shhh, everything's fine now," he said soothingly. He brushed the hair out of my eyes and tucked it behind my ear.

"You, Aubany Winters, are an amazing girl," he whispered. "I cannot believe you actually swam through the ocean to get to me, risked everything to try and save me, and even took a knife for me," he said. "Whoever said you weren't strong is a real idiot."

"I think *you* were the one who said that originally," I said, with a small smile.

"Then I am the idiot who doesn't deserve you," he whispered. "But I've fallen way too deeply in love with you to let you go, so you might just have to put up with me."

"I'd be more than happy to put up with you, Ryan," I replied.

His gaze met mine and it was filled with such intensity that, if I wasn't already laying down, I would have swooned.

"Why did you do all that for me?" he asked.

"Because I love you, Mr. Snarkypants," I replied with a grin.

He laughed, and his eyes lit up with happiness.

"Mr. Snarkypants, huh?" he asked teasingly.

I smiled at him, and he squeezed my hand.

"But, seriously," I said, my smile wavering, "Miley Cyrus?"

"Shut up," he grinned. "You loved it."

"Did I really? Maybe it was your song choice that made me pass out," I teased. I was joking, but I think I hit a nerve because Ryan frowned.

"God, I was so worried I lost you, Aubs," he said, looking serious again. "I was so scared."

"Yeah? Well, you kind of scared me, too. Don't *ever* lock me in a bathroom and disappear for two days ever again."

"I promise," he whispered, leaning over to kiss my forehead.

I felt like Ryan was my anchor, keeping me safe. Through all of these unbelievable situations, he had been by my side to help me. And he still was. I now truly believed I couldn't live without him.

"Oh, by the way," Ryan said, giving me a grave look, "Savannah is ready to kill you. She's *literally* outside waiting to kill you."

"Oh . . ." I trailed off. I could only imagine how she felt after I ditched her. "Yeah, okay, send her in."

"I hate to leave you even for a second, but I think this conversation needs a little privacy," Ryan added, getting to his feet. "But if she *does* actually try to kill you, just call out to me."

I laughed. "I think I'll be fine," I told him.

He gave me one last lingering look before heading out the door.

Savannah appeared in the doorway a few moments later. Her eyes were stormy grey, and she glared at me.

"You're in big trouble, Missy," she told me. She marched over and hugged me.

"I'm sorry, Savannah," I said. "But the note told me to come alone so I—"

350

"I don't care what it said," she cut in. "You almost *died*! You should have told me so we could have formed a better plan! Are you crazy or something? Swimming over to the island like that?"

"I'm sorry," I said again.

She sat by my side.

"Alex told me that part of it was trading yourself for him. Because of you, he was able to come back safely," she said. "I really owe you for that. Ryan, too."

"You're my friends. I'd help you no matter what," I said with a smile. She looked misty eyed now.

I frowned suddenly. "What happened to Courtney?"

Savannah shrugged. "We don't know. She got on her boat and left. No one's heard from her since. You've been out for nine hours."

"Nine?" I gasped.

"Yeah. Ryan didn't leave your side once during those nine hours. I had to bring him chips from the vending machine just so he didn't pass out."

I felt a fuzzy feeling in my chest and smiled.

Savannah ruffled my hair playfully.

"Well, now that I've yelled at you and thanked you, I'd better let you rest. I'll be back later," she said.

Savannah got up, then stopped.

"By the way, Alex says thank you, too."

"Tell *Alex* thank you," I replied. "I owe him my life."

"Will do," Savannah promised, before heading out the door.

I had to pause for a moment, as I thought back to Courtney stabbing me. To what she'd said to Ryan.

Don't you remember me, Ryan?

I pondered her words for a moment—it just seemed. . . odd. But then again. . . she *was* crazy.

Wasn't she?

I was drawn out of my thoughts when Ryan peered his head in.

"Can I come back in or do you want to be alone?" he asked.

"I want you with me," I replied.

He smiled and came back over to me. I took hold of his hand, drew him close, and kissed him gently.

"I missed you," I whispered, my hands slipping around his neck. He leaned closer and nuzzled into my neck.

"I missed you too," he whispered. He sat by my side and we cuddled for a long time.

~

Over the next few days, I had to stay in my room and recover. I received a visit from Josh and Renee, who had finally been informed about what had been going on and were angry at us both for keeping it quiet.

"You could have died!" Renee cried. "Did either of you think about that?"

"In our defence, we spent a *lot* of time in situations that *made* us think about that," Ryan replied.

Renee glared at him in a way that warned him not to make jokes.

"I have a good mind to pack us all up and leave the island right now," Josh added.

I didn't want to leave yet, but I wasn't in any position to protest.

Renee turned to me.

"Aubany, I have to call your father and tell him about this, so be expecting a phone call from him," she said.

I nodded.

In the end, the Ruperts decided to stay, seeing as Courtney had disappeared and there didn't seem to be any more signs of trouble.

Over the next few weeks, I recovered at a steady pace, and was finally able to do activities again.

My fear of the ocean was fading rapidly. After swimming to another island, there wasn't much left to be scared of, so Ryan took me out on jet skis and we even tried kayaking again, which went much better than the first time.

On our last day on the island, Ryan and I spent the day at the lagoon, splashing around and laughing with Savannah and Alex. At one point, Ryan led me over to the waterfall cave that was hidden behind the jungle vines. He pressed me against the cave wall and kissed the hell out of me.

"So . . . we go home tomorrow," he said finally, wrapping his arms around my waist.

"And my parents come back from California the day after," I added.

"Please don't tell me this is going to be one of those things where we break it off after the vacation's over," he said.

"Are you kidding me?" I asked. "Ryan, you have changed my life. You helped me overcome my fear of the ocean, and you saved my life on countless occasions.

"What we've been through together doesn't even come close to normal couples."

I took a deep breath and felt like it was time to tell him what I'd been thinking for weeks.

"Ryan, I'm completely in love with you . . . and I couldn't imagine my life without you. I don't *want* to go back to the life I lived before you came into it."

A smile formed on his lips. "Good . . . because there's something I want to ask you," he said. "I feel like I've been in love with you for my whole life. No other girl I've been with compares to you, and now that I *finally* have you . . . I want to do this the right way.

It's occurred to me that I still haven't asked you to be my girlfriend . . . I've been waiting for a really special moment to come along but . . . well, I feel like *every* moment with you is special."

I thought back, and realised he was right.

"So . . . are you asking?" I said, a smiling forming on my lips.

"Do you want to be my girlfriend?" he asked, looking hopeful.

"Only if you'll be my boyfriend," I replied play-fully.

He pretended to think about it. "I dunno . . ." he trailed off.

I whacked his arm and he laughed.

"Alright, fine," he said teasingly.

We kissed again, and I wrapped my arms around his neck. I felt completely anchored to him.

It hadn't occurred to me until now what life was going to be like back home. With Ryan and I together . . . everything was going to change. We had similar friend groups at school—meaning some of my friends knew some of his friends and the group was loosely connected in one way or another. With us together, it was going to grow even *more* connected.

I knew Melissa was going to have a thing or two to say about that, or about Ryan in general—considering she'd grown up listening to me rant and complain about him, and now I'd gone and fallen in love with him.

But . . . it didn't matter. They could say what they wanted. It wasn't going to change anything. Ryan and I had been through too much to go back to how we used to be.

"Are you glad you came on this vacation?" he asked softly. "Even with all the Courtney drama?"

When I first arrived on the island, my answer might have been something like "Hell no!", but now, as I looked at the person who had become as important to me as the salty air I breathed, I found myself saying, "This was the best vacation *ever*."

P.S.Malcolm

SNEAK PEEK!

read the prologue and first chapter of book two:

SURVIVING SPRING BREAK WITH RYAN RUPERT

PROLOGUE

"I'm hungry!" Aubany whined, like the little brat she was.

Trailing behind her parents as they hiked over a decaying, fallen log, she looked positively miserable.

The sight filled me with the richest delight.

"Seriously? You ate like, *two hours* ago!" I replied.

The leaves under my feet crunched as I walked.

"If you eat any more, you'll get all fat! Then you'll look like a balloon!"

Aubany shot me a dirty look, before whipping her head towards her Mom—her red hair flying in the process. She stomped her foot.

"*Mom!* Ryan's being mean again!"

"Oh, for pity's sake, you two, would you cut it *out*?" Mrs. Winters scolded, looking at the two of us over her shoulder.

She wore a huge backpack, and she had to peer over it. "You've both done nothing but bicker for the entire trip!"

I saw Aubany say something under her breath and fold her arms over her chest, but Mrs. Winters didn't see it.

Up ahead, my parents were taking photos with Mr. Winters with their brand new *Nikon D80* camera.

My Mom spotted us coming up the hiking trail, and her eyes shined with excitement.

"Ryan! *Smile!*" she sang, pointing the lens towards me.

I grinned, and the shutter went off.

She then took a picture of Aubany, who was still pouting.

We'd been walking for what seemed like a million years. There hadn't been much to look at apart from trees, so when Dad announced that he could see something up ahead, my heart began to race with excitement.

"Look!" he said, pointing through the bristly pine trees.

We all peered through the dense forestry, and made out what appeared to be a cabin. Dad took a step towards it, intending to go and check it out.

"Honey, that's someone's property!" my Mom scolded, pulling Dad back. "We shouldn't pry!"

The four adults continued onward, bickering about being *adventurous*, and I was about to follow them but I noticed Aubany sitting on a rock, pulling off her shoe. I couldn't help but roll my eyes.

"Come *on*, Aubany!" I said. Couldn't she wait until we got back to rest her feet?

"There's a rock in my shoe!" she protested, shaking her sneaker up and down really hard. I sighed, and decided to wait for her. The last thing we needed was for her to get lost.

Making a face, I looked around as I waited. I took a look at the cabin again, and was surprised to see a girl standing there. . . *staring* at me.

The girl continued to watch us, and I got an uncomfortable feeling.

"Hurry up, Aubany, or I'm leaving without you," I said with a shaky voice, wanting to catch up to my parents. The girl's creepy stare was making me worried.

"Just *wait*!" Aubany whined ignorantly, tying her shoelaces. I was scared, so I kept watching "Strange Girl". She hadn't moved one bit, she just kept staring. What a *weirdo*!

"There!" Aubany announced, jumping up from the rock.

Finally! I grabbed her by the arm and tugged hard. Ignoring her protests, I dragged both of us away, before walking again like before.

Maybe it sounds funny, but something wasn't right about that girl, and I wasn't hanging around to find out what.

CHAPTER ONE
Aubany

Class could not go any slower. I tapped my pen on the desk irritably, unable to contain my energy. I'd been pumped since the beginning of the week, when it had finally hit me.

The holidays were here!

It had been a year and a bit since my last vacation, to Nula Island. Although it hadn't been a dream vacation, it still changed my life dramatically.

Now, I have two new wonderful friends who keep in contact frequently through text and Skype. We met Savannah and Alex on the island, and they currently reside in Miami, but that isn't the best part.

I have the most *amazing* boyfriend ever, and it's all because of that trip.

Beside me was my best friend since first grade, Melissa Carter, who shot me an annoyed look for tapping the pen repeatedly.

I ceased the action, plastering a sheepish expression on my face.

Unlike myself, she *enjoyed* English. In fact, I think she just enjoyed school in general. She wanted to become a lawyer one day, and she was aiming for Harvard University.

I was completely exhausted after studying for finals all semester. Melissa, her boyfriend Lewis, and my boyfriend Ryan all shared the same sentiment, so we'd decided to spend our Spring Break at Lewis' lake house. None of us had been there, but we'd heard it was really nice. Situated out of town, it was dead peaceful, and there were plenty of opportunities for bonfires and hanging out. It sounded perfect after a stressful semester.

All thoughts of an exciting, fun-filled trip vanished when my teacher, Mrs. Denners, began to proceed down the aisle.

That could only mean one thing.

I grimaced, wanting to bury my head in my hands.

"So, I want you to spend your break doing these tasks I've prepared for you," Mrs. Denners said, handing out a sheet of paper to each of us. I heard groans echo throughout the class, and even I suppressed a grunt of disapproval as a sheet was placed down in front of me. The entire span of the paper, from top to bottom, was packed with preparation research questions for next semester's unit.

However, not even a sheet of homework could permanently dull everyone's excitement for the holidays, and when the bell *finally* rang, my classmates energetically jumped up and made for the door, laughing and chatting excitedly.

I grudgingly slipped the paper into my bag as I joined the horde.

Melissa and I shuffled through the crowded halls to our lockers to gather what we needed before we headed home.

Melissa's locker was closer to the front entrance, so we went to mine first, which was all the way at the back of the school.

"Don't forget that we're leaving at seven *sharp* tomorrow," Melissa reminded me, as I shoved all the books I didn't need into the locker.

"Oh, you don't have to *remind* me. The idea has been plaguing me all week," I replied.

As excited as I was for the trip, I didn't understand *why* we had to leave so early!

"Blakesky isn't that far away. We'd still get there by nightfall if we left around lunchtime."

Melissa gave me a pointed look.

"You sound like you want to put the trip off," she stated, eyeing me curiously.

I sighed. "It's not that," I began. "I just like sleeping in, and this is the first time in *months* that I haven't had to work an early weekend shift," I admitted.

I'd been working as a barista for almost a year now, and I *loved* it—free coffee, chats with the regulars, and making the latte art look *superb*. It *did* mean I worked long weekend shifts, though. "It would be nice to be able to sleep in, you know, just *once*."

Melissa rolled her eyes. "You can sleep in the car. We've got to leave early because Lewis wants to clean the place up when we arrive. It hasn't been visited in years. The last thing he'll want to do is clean everything if we get there late at night."

Well, I'd known it would be impossible to change her mind from the start, but at least I tried.

With a woeful sigh, I shut my locker and turned to head towards the school entrance, only to run into a tall, built body of muscle. I looked up.

"Geez, someone's eager to see me," Ryan teased, as he steadied me.

He grinned a cocky grin, and my expression of despair instantly melted into a smile as I wrapped my arms around him. I sank into his warmth and inhaled his familiar scent. A sense of security wrapped around me, like a blanket.

Melissa coughed, which brought me back to my senses, and I reluctantly stepped away from Ryan. Melissa's gaze was one of steel as she eyed the two of us disapprovingly.

"You may need to see that this one gets out of bed on time tomorrow," Melissa told Ryan coldly.

P.S.Malcolm

I would have shrunk away from such a gaze, but Ryan didn't seem fazed. In fact, he smirked at her.

"Don't worry. I'll turn the air conditioner up so it's freezing and pull the covers off of her, then lure her downstairs with coffee beans," he replied, and my eyes widened in protest.

"Don't you *dare!*" I said, the very thought of the situation making me shiver. "You may be my neighbor, but that doesn't mean you can break into my house in the early morning!"

"Why not? I've broken into your bedroom on countless occasions," he replied with a wink, and I flushed red.

Melissa made a disgruntled noise and said, "*Okay*, well, I'm going to head off now. I'll see you both tomorrow, *bright and early!*"

"Of course, *Your Majesty*," I replied, with a hint of sarcasm, as she flipped her midnight black hair over her shoulder and headed through the thinning crowd.

Melissa still wasn't happy about my relationship with Ryan. As the closest person who had grown up with me over the years, she'd watched him bully me time and time again. Then, one summer, I disappear for six weeks, and we come back skipping and holding hands like the past seventeen years never happened.

Melissa didn't approve, and she hasn't forgiven Ryan for his misdeeds yet. She almost didn't forgive *me* for letting him become such a prominent part of my life. But the decision I made was mine alone to make, and that thought comforted me.

I turned my attention back to Ryan, and just by looking at him I knew it was best decision I'd made so far.

"Did you get any homework to complete over the break?" I asked.

"Nope," he replied, his grin growing wider.

My eyes narrowed with jealousy.

"You're so lucky. I'll probably have to do mine on the trip tomorrow, otherwise I just *know* I'll forget about it."

"Just don't do it. Be a *rebel*, Aubs," he teased, and I resisted the urge to swat at him.

"You're a bad influence," I scolded, as we began to walk through the halls.

"You're the *thrill seeker* in this relationship," he reminded me, and I knew it was a joke, not a taunt.

Everything had flipped upside-down compared to what it used to be between us. What was once intended to be harmful had become the foundation of our relationship.

And it was a foundation that was going to last . . . right?

book two coming soon

P.S.Malcolm

ACKNOWLEDGEMENTS

Thank you to my parents, who support me in everything I do. Without you, I could not have gotten this far.

Thank you to Izzy, both Laura's, Lara, both Ashley's, Maddi, Mark, Zac, Emily and Jordan, for your support in the years that I wrote this book. Thank you to Tyler, who gave me courage. Though with me no more, you left me with so much.

Thank you to Amy for your *amazing* editing skills, to Jesh, for the stunning cover, and to Alina for the lovely map.

And lastly, thank you to *you*, The Reader, for picking up a new author, and reading my book to this very page.

P.S.Malcolm

ABOUT THE AUTHOR

P.S.Malcolm is the author of the *Starlight Chronicles Series* and the *Ryan Rupert Series*. She is a tea enthusiast, cat lover, and floral fanatic with a deep passion for writing stories.

She grew up in the tropics of Australia, close to the beach and surrounded by the bush.

Her other works, personal endeavors, and social media links can be found on her website:

psmalcolm.com